Maureen: After and Before

By

John Toft

to Sheena Barnes with all best wishes from John Toft.

Maureen: After and Before

© John Toft 2009

Whirley Lowe
Foxt
Staffs ST10 2HR

ISBN 978 - 0 - 9563741 - 0 - 3

Typeset in 9pt Aster New and printed in England
by PhotoPrint (Leek) Ltd
71, Haywood Street, Leek, Staffordshire ST13 5JH
www.photoprintofleek.co.uk
01538 384482

Printed in Great Britain by the MPG Books Group,
Bodmin and King's Lynn

Maureen: After and Before

✦

"But you never got married - you liddle waynker".

He cringed as much from the Australian accent as from the accusation. How, having no memory, had she remembered that? And this small crazy world had stopped to listen. No wonder - hearing a well-dressed elderly gent. called "a wanker"! Activity in the room ceased, all clatter and chatter, as the inmates and their warders made varying sense of what they had heard. It jolted him out of somnolence, the state he usually found himself in when visiting people in hospital. Trying to think of pleasant things to say always made him tired; it was like talking to the deaf. Here they were all either deaf or daft or both. The question was, would they be better off dead? But there was no choice, or - it amounted to the same thing - they did not know what choice was.

This grim building had once housed the Poor and the Little Sisters who took care of them on God's behalf. Now they did it on behalf of the Health Authority: it had become a "residential home" for the demented. A dwindling residue of nuns in "modern" dress had stayed behind to help. Not only had the distinctive look of the Little Sisters disappeared but so had the distinctive view from the front windows at one of which he was now sitting with Maureen. Gone was the place where his father had worked, the steel foundry which had seemed indestructible and made the city's sky, like his father's politics, permanent red. The old politics had gone the way of the old industry. Gone, way back, was the building where his mother had worked, Josiah Wedgwood's manufactory with its cupola'd belfry. Gone were the colliery's skeletal silhouettes and the biggest greyest gasometer in Europe. In their place glittered a designer water feature surrounding restaurants and multiscreen cinemas. Yet two bespired churches still perched above the pit quarry which now cosily accommodated DIY stores. Would religion still be sending its pinpricks of prayer into the sky in the year 3000? Would there be nuns?

Maybe Maureen's remark was not an accusation, after all, but a statement of fact or an expression of envy. But how could she, in her state, express anything?

"No, I never got married," he laughed. "And it was all because of you."

He tried to hold her eyes so that he could see what effect his words would have on her, but she had already forgotten her own and was busy doing up the buttons of her cardigan and then undoing them because she had missed one. She kept on missing one. From time to time her head drooped forward and her nose might have reached the floor, had he not, imitating the nun's retrieval action, uncurved her and laid her head against her pillow. The others, mainly women and just a few men - but what was the difference at their age and in their state? - were in various stages of droop, some sleeping, some lolling, some trawling the air with wondering fingers, none watching the hyperactive images on the TV screen.

"Shall we go for a little walk?" he suggested, with a view to keeping her upright.

"Where to?"

It was a fair question. "Along the corridor" hardly seemed inviting, so.

"Round and about," he airily offered.

"I don't want to go round or about."

"Well, let's go to Selham Park."

That, of course, was out of the question, but she seemed to start up at the name, and once she was on her feet she let him steer her along the corridor where a young male administrator was seated at a computer transcribing notes and ignoring the madness going on around him: that was for the nuns to deal with. He could have been an actor in a TV soap. Everybody was actor or audience now, on a screen or at a screen. Soon everybody would be sitting at screens watching each other sitting at screens. Nobody would do real jobs any more, except the dying handful of celibate females, who had to soothe and sometimes manhandle the patients and wheel them to the eternally swishing and gurgling toilets.

He walked Maureen along the corridor and back, taking care not to breathe too deeply in case the inevitable pee smell that met his nostrils might be coming from her. She seemed not to see the military-style gentleman who was carefully placing imaginary goods on imaginary shelves, or the genteel old lady who stood and uttered obscenities at a door on which a notice read NO UNAUTHORIZED PERSONS BEYOND THIS POINT. How could the patients know they were unauthorized if they didn't even know they were persons? Yet these had been people like Maureen, with decent, rational and meaningful lives behind them. He had once shared in hers, as others had shared in theirs. Now they were back to infancy, but without the fresh flesh of childhood. They had no future and had lost their past.

Yet she knew he had not married. How - why - had she known that, when she didn't seem even to know who he was? Did he know who she was? He only had the nuns' word for it. Nothing of this staring-eyed puffy-fleshed uncontrolled carcase reminded him of the Maureen he once knew. And loved. The only human female, apart form his mother, he had loved with a love that was more than just fond affection.

"I want to go home," she suddenly wailed. " I want to go back on the boat."

His heart clenched. Which boat did she mean? Her grandad's barge or the ship to Australia? So there was a vestige of memory. But so far back. So far away, perhaps beyond even their shared past.

"He'll be meithered to death about me."

"Who?"

"Who d'you think?"

"But he's -" useless to say "dead", since he whoever he was was clearly not dead to her, so "Yes, I'll take you home then," he sighed.

"Home" was now a cell with en suite facilities. He pushed open the tall heavy door. Patients could not get in or out on their own. The room was narrow and high, its architectural austereness compromised by the "personal" bits and pieces scattered about, soft toy animals, framed rural scenes, perfumed feminine niceties, and a frameless mirror with flowers and butterflies around its edge. That mirror! Now he knew that this was indeed his Maureen. His heart clenched at the sight of his own aged features framed in the flowers.

He glanced through the patient's file that had been left on the dressing table. It seemed casual, if not careless. But what the hell? She wouldn't read it and, if she did, she wouldn't know it was about her.

"It says here 'record bowel movement'. Is that a world record or just your personal best?" That would have given her a good laugh once. But now all she did was lift her skirt above her knees, showing slabs of flesh. He wished he did not find it so distasteful.

"No, I never got married," he said to change the subject, though he realised that he wasn't really changing it. "And it was all your fault, you know." He laughed to show that he was being gallant. Immediately he regretted what he had said. She stared into space. Then

"They know nowt about it," she said, her head lolling again towards the floor.

"About what?"

"About what?"

"What don't they know about?"

"You know. That business -"

"Marriage?"

"Not just that. You know – ." She grimaced and waved her hand, then took a deep sighing breath as if having to spell out the obvious to an idiot. "The birds and the wotsits - you know what I mean -"

He nodded, wondering what the word "meaning" meant to her now. The experts said that the past remained deep underground though recent events faded like dew. So he had come in the hope of excavating a sealed chamber in her brain, a place where she was still a girl and he a boy. But how far back did one have to go?

"Ray," he said. "You were married to Ray - remember? What happened to him?"

"Who?"

"Your Ray - Ray Devlin."

"Devlin? Married?" She repeated the words mechanically as if they belonged to a foreign language she was just beginning to learn.

"To Ray - Ray, your husband."

She frowned in the effort to understand. Then,

"Ooh - dead - duck!" she cried.

In this part of the world, he reminded himself, "duck" was a term of endearment, so perhaps she was making sense after all, saying "Dead, duck." But her tone was harsh and impersonal and forbade further probing. Was Ray really dead? Did she know or didn't she? Did the name mean anything at all? Her attention was now fixed on the auxiliary who was bringing her an afternoon cuppa with, "Sugar, shug? Ooh no, I'm forgetting you're sweet enough, aren't you, presh?"

Maureen gave a wonderful smile. The same banalities must have been uttered day in day out, but they made her smile as his unique visit had not.

"You can get one of my best cups out of the china cabinet for wotsisname here."

"Oh no," he said, looking round for the non-existent cabinet, "I'm alright."

"Tea's only for the patients, darling." The auxiliary winked and sloshed the tea into an institutional cup and put it beside Maureen.

"I know. It's quite O.K." Who, he asked himself, would want to drink from those cups any way?

But at least it gave him his chance to get away. She had her drink to take all of her concentration now. Even so, she spilt tea down her chin on to her frock. It lay untouched, unfelt, an orange brown blob on the puckered skin round her collarbone.

"I'll be seeing you," he said and, suddenly remembering something - it had been her favourite song way back in the 1940's - he softly crooned, " - in all the old familiar places."

For a moment there was a flicker of something - not quite recognition - in her eyes. She smiled, but then her tea slopped again and she became obsessed with the effort of pushing her cup back into its saucer. He feebly went on half-humming the song, but her face was turned from him in concentration on the cup. She no longer knew that he was there, and he had already run out of things to say.

Of course, he told himself, I shan't be seeing her again, but the song pursued him past the nurse's desk to the exit,

"I'll be seeing you in every lovely summer's day" past the young administrator who was now exchanging camp banter with a burly porter wheeling a flat-out crone into her cell. "I'll always think of you that way " past the nuns' chapel which was now 'kept open for quiet rest and reflection'.

"I'll find you in the morning sun" and so on through the hospital grounds to the car park, where, not having used up his allotted time, he offered his ticket to a sharply dressed woman emerging from a posh four-by-four. She looked at him as if he were a sex offender. In fact she had parked in a place marked "Staff Only". As he turned away in confusion, he wondered if her suspicions would have been confirmed had he voiced the words that sang in his head:

"I'll be looking at the moon but I'll be seeing you."

He hadn't revisited his home town to see Maureen Devlin. That had been Graham Greatbatch's idea. The main business had been his father's funeral. Along with his brother, Jimmy, he had seen Dad off to the incinerator. The mourners shook hands with the vicar and thronged the April-rinsed courtyard. Some gave priority to the bereaved, others to greeting relatives they hadn't seen since the last funeral, while the blatant few checked that their floral tributes were clearly on display.

It was all wrong of course. There should have been no flowers, no service, no vicar, no fuss. Jack's father had been a strict atheist and socialist all his adult life. Religion was strictly for the fearful and feeble-minded. And now his own sons had proved their feeble-mindedness by letting the undertakers have their capitalistic way. Jimmy was a not very well man with a wife who said "if you can't do a thing properly, then don't do it at all". As not doing it at all wasn't an option, Jimmy had numbly nodded when the undertaker asked, "C. of E.?, Standard rites? Flowers? Cars? A notice in The Sentinel? A modest reception?" Jack had the excuse of living "down south" but had given the same numb assents over the phone. It was, like so many turns in his life, out of his hands. Like not having married.

The all-purpose clergyman, brought in for those without any particular faith, moved on to the next corpse. The organ swelled and the processing plant swung back into action. Exchanging shrugs with his brother over the politically undesirable fuss, Jack turned to deal with friends and family he had not seen, as people were saying, "for yonks".

"See how long is it you've lived down south now? " Graham Greatbatch asked. He was satisfied and prosperous in his retirement, as well he might be, having run a string of petrol stations. But his eyes were still those of a boy: button-like, dark and merry.

"Forty years. But I still think of the Potteries as home. God knows why."

"You wouldn't want to come back? You like it in Sussex?"

"Well, of course it's nice and handy for London and the Continent."

"Oh yes, we're all Europeans now, aren't we?"

"But you never really get away from your home town." God, he thought, how death brings out the clichés. "The grime gets ingrained in your soul."

"It's a lot cleaner now."

"Yes, I can see that. But the old character's gone."

"Some might think it's better without that character."

"I dare say I'm letting nostalgia run away with me. So many memories."

Graham looked at him, black button eyes a-twinkle.

"Remember that time in Molds' loo?"

"Unforgettable." He had not thought anybody else would remember. It had seemed an aspect of his abnormal single state that he never forgot it.

"Talk about the innocence of children! One of us has forgotten though."

"Who?"

"Who else? There were only the three of us."

"You mean Maureen Foster, as she then was?"

He had not thought of her for a long time, but now it seemed the name had always been there, waiting to be uttered.

"She's gone childish."

"Childish?"

"Senile you know. Demented."

"Maureen? But I thought - she's only a bit older than me."

For some reason he didn't want to say the exact difference - five years.

"She's my age - remember? We're seventy now."

"Well, I'm catching up - I've just become an OAP."

"Ah, but you'll never overtake us."

"Yes, but I might drop out before you - or Maureen. Any way, seventy's not old now we're all living longer."

"You don't have to be old to be senile, you know."

"Isn't she in Australia?"

"She came back."

"She? What about her husband?" Jack pretended to search his memory for a name he knew well. "Wasn't it Ray Devlin?"

Graham shrugged.

"They say he was a bugger to her. He led her a dance in Australia - I don't know. But look - why don't you go and visit her while you're here? You might just jog her memory. You were her little darling in those days."

It was Jack's turn to shrug.

"What would be the point? I mean, if she doesn't remember anything."

"She can remember some things way back. It could be just the short term memory that's gone. Go on - give her a surprise. It might shock her back to life."

"It might finish her off."

"Probably the best thing in the circumstances. Who'd want to live like that?'"

Jack looked into the western sky spreading green and rust washes over the canal where Maureen's grand-dad's barge had plied, and over the hill which hid the now strange city. So she was back here, the magical girl of sixty years ago? Senile. And his mother was scattered in the Garden of Rest. And his father, having been rendered to ash in the incinerator, was awaiting dispersal. A world had gone. But why did irrelevant bits of it still survive? Himself, for instance..

Jack followed his brother along the Avenue of Remembrance. There, at the end, where nothing was allowed to stand above ground level, Jimmy said they would eventually scatter Dad's dust, though "Whether it'll really be his, God alone knows". Dad wouldn't mind though, being scornful of graveyards and memorials. The Crematorium, decent sensible thirties modern, with phalanxes of poplars, squared rose-beds and carefully signposted areas of committal, was the epitome of what the twentieth century had done to al the centuries that had gone before. It said it all, and said it on the edge of every city in the land. It comes to this: the carefully raked rose-bordered cinder track. Was that why some people let their minds go before their bodies, to shut out the absurdity of ending? This particular ending happened to coincide with the century's.

I was trapped in a balloon of skin. The balloon stretched over bones that groaned with pain. It grew bigger till it stifled me. Then it broke. Struggling to escape from thick webs of skin, I saw my father at the far corner of a long room. He wore a trilby and looked at me as a stranger might, his face a mask.

I awoke screaming. Dadda was there, but now he rescued me from the nightmare he had haunted. I saw the familiar collarless old shirt he slept in, and the silhouette of his legs against the candlelight. Jimmy was grumpily nudging me awake.

"It's all right," Dadda was calling. "There, there, it's all right."

He walked up and down with me in his arms till the horror went. Cold now, we climbed into bed with Mamma, who sighed. Dadda put his arm round me, drawing me to his stomach. So we went back to sleep happily.

The next moment Mamma was getting up to go to the pot-bank. I moved into her space, smelling her turpentine smell. Dadda and I rolled together, he enfolded me and I smelt his smell, of sweat and cigarette tobacco. He loved me then, with playful caresses: it was the only love I ever wanted.

At last, time not exerting itself in any way to pass, the long day began, still with Dadda, always with Dadda. There was breakfast, pobs of bread in sugared hot milk. Then I performed the Big Grunt on the jerry because our lavatory was down the yard and too deep and dangerous for me. But my father did his grunt there and kept the door open to watch me playing. He always smoked while he grunted. Sometimes, when his money had run out, he rolled bits of string into paper and smoked them. When the lavatory got blocked he had to poke an iron spear down the long wide tunnel into the faraway underground, to make the ducket turn over. I liked to see the dripping slime at the end of the spear, but I ran away when it was swung round.

Then I was washed, and watched Dadda wash, in the back kitchen sink. I liked his shaving strop and the worn bristles of his brush and his way of scraping round his moustache. Occasionally he would shave off the moustache, and we hated it because he looked reduced, or, as Mamma put it, "he looks what he is". I did not want him to look what he was.

We walked through the park to the Labour Exchange, by the clock house with its green wooden veranda, down the ball-and spike-crested steps to the bandstand, where flattened chairs were stacked for Sunday, over the canal bridge and round the bowling-green to the pedestalled water fountain. Dadda lifted me to press its brass plug and I took an iron-tasting draught from the chained and clanking ladle.

When Dadda found a forgotten sixpenny bit in his pocket he would take me rowing on the lake. He fancied himself with the sculls. I trailed a finger in the water to catch at stalks, blossom and feathers, and stared the swans out.

When there was no sixpence to be found we headed straight for the dole queue. We were all men together there, as the women had to form a queue of their own at a different door. Most of the time was spent in the street outside shuffling along the sooty wall and under the opaque windows of the Labour Exchange. Clerks asked curt questions to humble the truculent. I was frightened because this would be one of those moments when my father, even with his moustache, would look what he was.

"Arsepokers," he called the clerks. He got his dole at last and his face relaxed. He put me on his shoulders and we moved on to the Municipal Library. We visited the Reading Room first where he scanned the racing page. He stood there with his pencil stub and a scrap of paper, on which would be inscribed in florid writing those strange names which the horses didn't know they bore.

Again it was men, only men in the Reading Room, and I was lost among legs, trousered ones and long spindly wooden ones. Newspapers were laid out full breadth under brass bars on desks which could only be stood at. The wooden legs tirelessly bore the brunt of the lecterns and the men leaning on them, while the trousered ones kept shifting in weariness or dissatisfaction. All I could hear was the waft of the pages and the wheezing of lungs, and everywhere was the singular Library smell of polish and disinfectant.

We moved on to the Lending Department. Standing below counter level, I could not see the faces of the librarians, but the tones of their whispers and my father's responses conveyed almost as many volumes as stood on shelves that reached the ceiling, all in the colours of library binding: sea green, dull red, mouse brown, mourning purple and deep-grained black, all mottled round the edges of the pages to mask the grubbiness of much fingering by the masses. What Dadda wanted was political and rarely fingered and always hard to get at, so then I watched the snooty assistant climb up his long thin ladder with its wide lean-to atop. I decided I should like to be a librarian, with the rubber-soled superior air of a schoolteacher or a minister of religion.

From the library Dadda's feet took us automatically to what he called "the shop", though it was only a house like the others in the street, no window display and no goods for sale, nothing legal or above board, just a coming and going of men, always men: smoking, coughing and spitting; moustached, cleanshaven or stubbled; shoed, booted or clogged. There was a mingling of smokers, infiltrated by yeast and the occasional whiff of spirits. I saw mainly trouser legs, clean and filthy and in between, shiny grey flannel or Prince of Wales check or potbank calico. And hands, reaching into pockets, lifting out watches, nose rag, cigarette packets, lighters, matchboxes, pipes, rolled pouches, little scraps of paper with the heart-quickening names on them, and much money - not mere coppers but half crowns, ten bob notes, even a white folded fiver. The faces that went with the legs and hands were just a blur, but I remember the man with a ledger like a long Bible under a wide green lampshade. That was where the smoke lingered, along with hopes, before fading. The man looked satisfied and sweaty and porkpie-fed.

Without me Dadda might have stayed there all day waiting for "the results", talking about horses and women with men, only men. He never backed a winner. I felt his droop and shamble as we turned away from the counter and were let out through the door that was kept manned against a police raid.

On the way home we called at the butcher's and got (on the slate, leaving Mamma to pay for it from her wages at the weekend) a thin piece of steak. I had to face the accusing stare of the great steer's head that jutted as if through the wall with the body still behind it, so real were those eyes, above the knife-clashing Mr Pye. There was the thick smell of blood, with an undertow of menthol, and in the sawdust on the floor were bits of unknown beasts. Snuff, said Dadda, had eaten Mr Pye's nose away. We ate his meat and the snuff ate his nose. Something, too, was at his lungs, for he often cleared his throat into a massive spittoon, wiping his walrus moustache with raw splodgy fingers. He cut up the bodies on an altar of dealwood, indelible red in its scrubbed grain. The hacked corpses swung from hooks, without identity. My eyes were always drawn to the pig products: trotters, giblets, brawn, bacon and sausages, festoons of them, black, green, pink and white, peppered, tomatoed, spiced and herbed, but even in this stylised state unmistakably porcine. The shiny skins reminded me of my nightmare balloon.

At home my father grilled our crimson beef to a salty blackness, then broke and grilled an egg on the same chipped enamel plate. We dipped our bread in it and Dadda pressed shreds of beef into my greasy golden mouthfuls. Then came the best moment of all. Dadda sank into his armchair and I climbed on top of him. I rode his legs to Banbury Cross or played Flyaway-Peter Flyaway-Paul with flakes of newspaper on licked fingertips. Soon he would begin to doze, my body splayed like a cat across his chest.

When I couldn't sleep I traced my fingers over his moustache and chin to feel the stubble, or I straightened the hairs curling up out of his shirt above the loose neck-line of the vest. Sometimes he would suddenly open his mouth and pretend to bite my finger. When he was really asleep I gazed at his shut face and snuggled down on his heaving diaphragm. We were so completely at one it seemed impossible that I should be excluded from his dreams. Then I lulled at last into my own.

I awoke to Mamma's return from the long day at the pot-bank where she decorated dishes at three-halfpence a dozen. Wearily she put out our tea which she had brought in with her - chips and sloppy peas or oatcakes to be wrapped round bacon and cheese. She frowned at Dadda's sprawling snoring form. Then Jimmy would breeze in from after-school play, like a dog drawn by its nose.

"I never got married and it was all your fault."

It wasn't Maureen's fault at all, of course, simply the consequence of his being who he was and the first people in his life being who they were. He hoped she hadn't taken any notice of what he said. There was a lot to be said for forgetfulness. It was his purgatory to remember things that needed to be forgotten. Maureen was now beyond remembering or registering anything, least of all a casual remark, even at the moment it was uttered. Any way, it was absurd to hold her responsible for his single state. Once she might have been flattered to think that she had stood in the way of his marrying. His words could have been interpreted as a romantic tribute – ah, if only it were that simple! In fact, it was so complicated that he felt a need to explain himself. But to whom? He had no descendants to appreciate a written record of ancestral life in a strange near-and-far-off world. Now, he suddenly realised, there was somebody to whom he had much to say. Ironic, therefore, that she would not be able to comprehend it.

Still, there was no harm in trying. He decided to stay on for a few days and visit Maureen till he had written their story. It would give him a reason for still existing. As a retired man on sufficient means, without progeny, without dependents, he had achieved as pure an existential freedom as it was possible to get. But he had found that very freedom self-defeating. He was no longer important to anybody. There was no particular reason for him to be "down south", or here or there or anywhere. The one place he had always wanted to avoid was his home town, but he realised he could bear it now because it wasn't the place he had known. It belonged to others, not to him.

And while he was here, he would visit Maureen again. He would bear that too. Old age, dementia, death, they had to be faced. Against all the odds he would address her. It wouldn't matter if he bored her to death or if his memory played him tricks. He could say anything he liked to her. Better than a psychiatrist, better that a priest, she couldn't use what he said as evidence against him. Besides, it might do her a good turn, as Graham Greatbatch put it. Perhaps something would get through to her, and if it didn't, at least he would have said it. After all, he would soon become senile himself one way or another and all would be lost. At present his memories were sharp and detailed; only what connected them was missing if there ever was a connection. There was so much that he needed to remind himself of. What an odd word "remind" now seemed. If only he could re-mind Maureen! Yet would she thank him for restoring what had maybe gone of its own accord? Would one want to relive the life that had already been sloughed off? And, with no possibility of her corroboration, how could he be sure he was, if not inventing it, at least making more of it than there had been? What had meant much to him was now nothing to her. Perhaps it never had been much to her. Married people had by definition fuller lives, more legitimate concerns.

Yet Graham Greatbatch had remembered that time in Molds' lavatory. There were others to address as well: the readership of the ancestral dead, the strewn and committed ash that lay all around him.

When he arrived at the "Home" a few days later with a brief history of his relationship with Maureen, ready to read to her, a nun told him she was sleeping "like a baby." The Irish eyes smiled behind their NHS spectacles and for a moment it was as if the virgin spinster had become a proud mother.

"But I expect she'll wake up for a visitor - we don't get many of those."

It wasn't clear whether the "we" meant Maureen only, or the whole institution. It would be understandable, if not forgivable, to stop visiting loved ones who no longer recognised, let alone loved, one in return.

"No, let her sleep. I'll sit here till she wakes of her own accord."

The nun seemed to approve of that. No doubt she had done a lot of sitting in her time, with the sick, the dying and the dead. Manfully she held the heavy door open for him and he slipped into the room. Maureen's face was bloated and bleary and her mouth dribbled. Yet for those very reasons it was like a baby's.

The quietness of a room where there are two people, one sleeping, one wakeful, seemed so different from what he was now used to: a room where there is one person alone. The breathing of the sleeper is so powerful that the person awake feels he should not be there or should be asleep also. The breathings are like echoes from another world which is forever closed to the wakeful. Maureen twitched and shifted, her face smiled, frowned and puckered, she gave a sigh now and then. Though he could not enter her world, or investigate it by empirical research, it was indisputably there. An inner life went on, separate from the body that lay like a sleeper in an air-raid shelter, massively rounded by extra clothes and immobilised by its own weight, briefly tunnelled away from the disasters of the waking world. He recalled nights in Fosters' air-raid shelter when he slept so between his mother's and Maureen's lither warmth. Outside, older men who were not fighting or working, sat smoking and murmuring, waiting for the bombers which rarely came that way. Inside, it was a world of women, with their young snuggling to their backs or bosoms. We must, he thought, have stunk like foxes, for one of the men, a veteran of the First War, came and sprayed a perfumed disinfectant in at the entrance to their earth.

Just as it was unlikely that those sleepers dreamed of war, so Maureen was almost certainly not dreaming of her dementia, since she could not, even in the so-called light of common day, perceive herself as being demented. Yet something was visibly going on for her. Surely it was impossible for a mind not to be working at all. Tranquillized as no doubt she was, she was far from being dead. A confused mind cannot be empty. Could it be that in her dreams Maureen was making contact with that childhood self he hoped to resurrect?

"Where are you, Maureen?" he whispered.

She did not respond.

Could this bloated body really be all there was of her? He was enough of a child of his time to believe that death was the full stop: no God, no immortal soul. But lately he had been brooding on questions which at university he had been taught to regard as pseudo-questions: God, life after death, the immortal soul. Those propositions were, of course, not inter-dependent, though most people seemed to think they were. There could be a Creator who denied immortality to his creations. Equally there could be an after-life without a god to preside over it. In his day as an undergraduate, it had been fashionable in the Philosophy Faculty to poke fun at "the Ghost in the Machine". Yet how insulting to our ancestors who spoke so freely of the soul. How offensive, too, to all the diseased brains and disabled bodies in the world, to say that only bodies and brains matter. There was a time, not so long ago, when saints and idiots and cripples were deemed special to God. Who would dare to deny it?

No, there had to be more to Maureen than this. Surely her memories came back to her in dream, no more fragmentary or distorted *than anybody else's. And perhaps the fragments could be re-assembled, would be indeed in another realm of being. Even as he framed these thoughts, the sleeper's body began to shake, its loose mouth to whimper. Thinking she might be having a fit or seizure he dashed to the door to fetch an attendant. But then he realised it was no more than a nightmare, which, as her thighs squirmed, she seemed almost to be riding. He dared not wake her, and when the ride was over, he was glad he had not tried to, for a look of ineffable happiness came over her face and she appeared a girl again. Could she have experienced orgasm? Did women of seventy still have orgasms? He did not know, and was annoyed with himself for not knowing. If he had been married it would have all been different. Should he touch her hand and bring her back to her fuddled consciousness and a world where the rational and irrational, the subjective and objective, were in endless contention? Surely, it was kinder to leave her in the coherence of her dream. Besides, he shrank from touching her.*

Maureen: After and *Before*

Deciding to tear up his neat, precise little essay on their childhood relationship, he was about to leave. But just at that moment a cleaner breezed in.

"She's such a dear old lady!" the domestic exclaimed as she busied about Maureen's room. Whereas the nuns referred to Maureen as a "girl", the ancillary staff saw her as antique. She now sat up in bed, smiling as the Hoover was whizzed around the floor. In between bouts of the horrible noise the domestic expatiated.

"She's so generous, she'd give anything to anybody. You only have to say you like something and she wants to give it you. I was just saying what a lovely mirror that is and she said take it, it's yours."

It was the mirror with the iridescent flowers and butterflies. He suddenly felt as though he were about to be bereft: he wanted to go on seeing the mirror on his visits, it belonged to the past he and Maureen shared with nobody else. And besides, he didn't like her being referred to as an old lady. Presumably they saw him as an old gentleman, even an old fart.

"I wonder if she took it with her to Australia."

"Where d'you say, duck?" The woman switched off the Hoover and leaned with her two red hands on it.

"Oh – " He had really been talking to himself. "To Australia."

"She never told me she'd been Australia - me and me 'usband went to Florida last summer," then, ignoring the man's unenthusiastic response, called more loudly in the direction of the bed, "-you never told me you'd been Australia, sweetheart. You are a dark horse, aren't you? When would that be?"

"Nineteen forty-eight" It was Maureen who spoke, seeming still half asleep. But she was spot on. Jack, who had been just about to

Maureen: After and Before

reply for her, was amazed.

"Nineteen forty-eight! Good grief, I wasn't even born then. I didn't know people went that far in them days. Did you have a nice time?"

"No." Maureen stared into distant space.

"It wasn't a holiday," Jack explained. She and her husband emigrated."

"Emigrated? They say it's all sunshine in Australia. Just like Florida - it's fabulous there. Why ever did you come back to this dirty 'ole and our rotten English weather?"

"She came to be with her mother who also became senile."

"Senile." Maureen echoed, trying to see distant time.

"We don't use that word here, do we, ducky? Confused's what we say - just a bit confused, that's all."

"Aren't we all?" he murmured at the woman's large behind as it disappeared into the bathroom. He wished he dared to shut the bathroom door so as not to see it bending and unbending at the bath and lavatory pan. Why, he asked himself, are working-class women so fat nowadays? And why, when they reach a certain age, do they all wear the same glasses and have the same hair-dos? Ugly. Ugly. While she was gone he went and looked at himself in the mirror. What he saw was ugly too, so different from the image of him it had held sixty years back. Different, too, was the image of Maureen in the background. Once upon a time she had bared herself to the glass to show off the paps forming on her chest.

She was so thrilled he felt resentful that paps would never grow on his. By rights, he thought, Maureen should give the mirror to me, only to me. Only I know what it means. Instead it would hang meaninglessly on the walls of this amiable uncouth woman among the bric-a brac of a hundred holidays. But then he smiled at his own absurdity. It would look even more out of place on his wall: it was as unacceptable to his educated taste as it was significant to his unchanged heart. This had happened before, with his parents' things, with their whole world, the place they came from and had brought him up in: loved and familiar things had become alien to him, and repulsive, in his quest for beauty and good tone.

"What d'you think I ought do?' The cleaning lady broke in on his thoughts.

"I'm sorry - about what?"

"That mirror. It isn't as if I could just put it in me pocket. I'd be seen carrying it off. We're not supposed to accept gifts from patients, though everybody does of course."

"No doubt they do."

"Then again, she doesn't need it - she's got the dressing-table. And it's no use to nuns now, is it?"

"I suppose not." Why the hell doesn't the woman clear off, he wondered.

"Besides, she really wants me to have it. As I told her, it takes me back. Me Auntie Florrie had one. It's what I call a real period piece - sort of thing you see on the Antiques Roadshow."

So that was it, not nostalgia but greed. He began to feel anger at this woman, who seemed all too typical of her kind.

"I don't suppose you'd take it out for me - they wouldn't suspect you - you could say she'd given it you -"

"Well, I really don't think -"

"Go on, please. She wants me t'ave it, don't you, darling?"

"What?"

"That mirror - you said so -"

"Who said so?"

"You did - last Thursday. Remember?"

"What did I say last Thursday?"

"You said this mirror's yours."

"It is mine."

"No, I mean - you said you'd give it me. Remember?"

"It's no use asking her if she remembers." Jack was surprised at his own sharpness. "Why can't you leave her in peace?"

"Oh - yes. I shouldn't have brought it up. I'm ever so sorry, duck."

The woman put her hand fondly over Maureen's. Maureen smiled beatifically. The woman was, as the local word had it, sneeped. She is really more gracious than I am., he thought.

"Don't forget that mirror I said you could have," Maureen called as the woman collected her cleaning materials and made for the door.

"I'll bring it out for you, "Jack said. "You can take it from me in the car-park."

The next time he saw Maureen, she complained.

"The staff in this hotel are a bunch of crooks. They help themselves to my best underwear, and d'you know that lovely mirror I had up there -" she pointed at the place on the wall where the mirror had hung - "it's gone. Don't ask me where. They told me this was a first-class place. Well, it isn't. And the manager doesn't come when you send for him."

"She's been going on and on about that mirror," the nun said when she came in. "I don't suppose you know anything about it, do you?"

"No," he said quickly, his cheeks flushing. Just at that moment he could not tell the truth, even to a nun. But, as she gave him a strange look, he guessed that somebody must have seen him bearing the wretched thing along the corridor.

Later, in the office, he confessed, explaining that he had not wanted to get the cleaning lady into trouble or to expose Maureen's memory-loss in front of her.

"It wouldn't have mattered," the nun sighed. "She'd soon forget that as well. I'll speak to Denise about it, so don't worry. This sort of thing is always happening."

When he came the next time, the mirror was back in its place. But when Denise came in, Maureen inquired brightly,

"Why didn't you take that mirror I said you could have?"

"I shall take it one day, sweetie, don't worry now."

"You mean when I'm a gonner."

"Well, you're not gone yet. Who knows, I might go before you."

"If you do, will you be there to meet me when I come?"

"Of course I will, my darling,"Denise said, taking Maureen in her arms and giving her a hug.

If only I could do that, Jack thought. If only I could be "there" for her. It seemed so much better than gazing at her with sympathy and weaving webs of words which she would never read.

Maureen: After and Before

When the war began everybody seemed to be on the march. My march was to school up the road. Dadda took me and left me there the day before he started work at the steel foundry. I watched him slip out by the glass-panelled door and into the corridor, his trilbied head moving along outside the high windows, with that look of the receding stranger seen in my nightmare. I yelled and wailed for him to come back but he didn't. Miss Peabody showed me a box of silvery sand and the playtime toys even though it wasn't playtime. But I went on wailing. The other children looked on, disapprovingly. The day when time began seemed as long as all the timeless days preceding it. But in the following days I came to love my personal hook in the cloakroom, my own enamel bowl, my own green and orange smock for painting, my own slate on which the chalk ran so softly and roundly as it created before my eyes the beauty of words and numbers. I even came to love the small pillow that replaced my father's chest for afternoon naps. Soon I was happy to play with shaven-headed boys and girls with slides and "nits" in their hair.

Especially girls. They had somehow more presence, were more complete. They were more like little women than boys were like little men. One was called Maylee Lu. One day when Miss Peabody smacked us for playing in the sand after playtime was over, I whispered, "Peabody by name and Peabody by nature."

I had heard my mother refer to people in this way and was glad our own surname didn't begin with "pea" or end in "bottom".

Maylee went into high-pitched giggles that could only be stopped by another smack, but every time we looked at one another we tittered. We became friends. Maylee's parents kept a laundry which stood halfway between our house and the school, so she would wait for me at the shop door and we went to school together. Maylee's mother waved us off. Though English, she was getting to look more and more Chinese, her skin yellowing, her fingers tapering, her cheekbones and even her voice heightening. Mamma said this was because she slept with Mr Lu. I wondered which of the three people – Dadda, Jimmy and Mamma - I alternately slept with I should grow to look like.

I wished I could sleep with Maylee so that I might look like her. Her little face with its fringe of black hair seemed perfect in its feline purity. I also wished my father ran a laundry with its scorched and steamy atmosphere, from which Mr Lu would emerge smiling like a sage from the joss-stick fumes of a temple.

One holiday I was uncertain which day school would be resuming and naturally went to consult Maylee. But there was no response to my knock at the house door. So I went round to the back door which opened into the laundry. I was allured and terrified by the damp hanging sheets and the boiling vats and the noise of drubbing and ironing. Suddenly Mr Lu loomed:

"Maylee out with mummy," he said.

My mouth opened, but at first no words would come out. Then

"I only wanted - " I stammered and stopped.

"What? What you want?"

I was so frightened I forgot what I wanted. Suddenly Mr Lu's long fingers gestured on the air and something mysteriously appeared between them. It was a Chinese sweetmeat which he handed to me. I did not know what to do with it.

"Taste. Taste." He licked out his tongue encouragingly.

I tasted. Then I thought for a moment, doubtful whether I liked the taste. It was so sweet and yet also so bitter. I kept on tasting and thinking and tasting again. I still didn't know whether I liked it. Then I remembered why I had come.

"It's Toysday!" Mr Lu most vehemently responded to my question.

"Toysday?"

"Toysday."

There was a pause as if the laundry itself was listening.

"Tuesday?" I ventured. "Or Thursday?"

"Toysday! Toysday!"

He nodded and I nodded too. He laughed and I laughed too. I was none the wiser but somehow Mr Lu made me feel very happy with the world. I wanted it to be toys' day every day.

At school Maylee and I did all that was permitted to a girl and a boy to do together. We sifted the silver sand, shared chalks and slates, cut Christmas trees out of gum-backed squares of green paper, wove raffia into warm-coloured patterns, slept on adjacent pillows and awoke smiling into each other's eyes. Even - though Miss Peabody smacked us for it - we exchanged straws halfway through the milk break and swopped Horlicks tablets for Zubes. The fact was, I now not only wanted to look like Maylee, I wanted to be her. Her plump soft body was a vessel of love, whose material form came in the shape of the Dolly Mixture she shared with me. I thought this love would go on forever. But then, dear Maureen, you came into my life.

I climbed the long yard wall in hope of seeing the new people who had just moved in next door. I saw a little old man sitting in the lavatory with his trousers dangling round his clogs. He waved and I waved back. I was pleased to note that his feet didn't touch the ground, as mine didn't when I sat on our pan. The old man inserted a clay pipe into his toothless mouth, puffed his sun-red wind-etched cheeks and hummed high up in his nose.

From then on the old man was often there when I climbed the wall. He seemed happy to spend hours just sitting. Sometimes he would hold conversations with my mother when she was hanging out washing. I brought my pals in to see "the old man humming with his trousers down".

One day a Big Girl came out of the house and called, "Granddad, Grom says you're to come in and stop fartarsing about."

So there you were. I was four and you all of nine. I immediately took to your gold-glinting brown hair, mischievous brown-black eyes and rousing manner. I was impressed, too, by your language and the way the old man obeyed you, tilting his lower half forward and putting his feet into the clogs. Hoisting up his trousers,

"Folla may," he said, "and I'll folla thay."

You looked at me and shrugged. Then you smiled. You had a dimple on either side of your lips.

"So are you coming in as well?" you asked as if this would naturally follow. It was the first of so many times I climbed over that wall, finding the footholds that would become worn with poking by my shoe. I trembled because the ground was lower on your side than on ours. It seemed a long way down, but you took me in your brown arms and I knew I was safe.

"Say M'reen," you corrected me when I called you, "More-in."

Inside the house Grom sat at the kitchen table, counting out her money, which was a mound of silver half crowns, florins, shillings, tanners and three-penny pieces like small wafery winter moons. She rejected pence and the new thick brassy bits, and I was glad because she sometimes gave them to you, and you bought something we could share. The money was kept in two red-spotted kerchiefs identical with the one round her husband's neck. I had never seen so much money all at one go, and it looked real, like a dragon's hoard, as a wad of notes never can. Grom was a benevolent dragon who, when she had counted to her satisfaction, kept the kerchief-bags on the chair behind her back, where, when she moved, they were heard grating and chinking as if her very bones were made of money.

"You daft bugger!" The dragon said when her husband came in at a mock gallop, smacking his haunches, as we did when playing cowboys and Indians. He stood before her, his foot pawing the rag rug and his head giving a shake and whinny.

The old woman turned to me as if she had known me all her life.

"Dosta want tak im wom wi thee?"

Having no granddad in our home, I nodded, though dubious about how my parents would react.

"I'll wrap him up in brine paper for thee. Dosta think tha cust carry im on thy ownyo?"

I nodded again, more dubiously.

"So 'ow much wou't give me for im? I'd want it in siller, tha knowst. He's wo'th a coupla bob."

"He's not having my granddad," you chimed in, and then stage-whispered at me, "Take no notice of her." You put a finger to your temple and made a screwing motion.

"No, I'm not, you cheeky a'porth. I've got me yead screwed on - unlike some."

Grom glanced sharply at Grandad whose hands made motions at his neck as if to lift his head off. I laughed.

"Don't encourage them," you warned me as if you were the grownup and they the children.

Granddad galloped out to do some more fartarsing about, and you showed me round the house as if it were a stately home. It was in form identical with but in content entirely different from ours. Although she was not at that moment there, your mother was clearly the dominant presence. Our rooms were dull with outdated handed-down bits of furniture. This place was full of new knickknacks. It had a Hollywood glamour, the glamour of women. It made me feel dissatisfied with the gender that had been assigned to me. A series of frocks hung from the picture rail, white, pink, yellow and polka-dotted, with puff sleeves and patent leather belts. Then, stacked under the sideboard, were as many shoes as one saw at the cobbler's, all ladies' and dainty, with the highest possible heels. You rummaged among them, a smell of leather and feet and perfume arose, and you selected two pairs, one red with bows, the other plain black but glossy - you called them "patent". You slid your feet into the black and tossed the red over for me to wear.

"They're three-'nd-'alfs," you said as if stating an important fact. This told me something about your mother. Mine took size fives.

We careered and clattered about the house then, like ladies at a thé dansant where the tea was laced with gin. In the middle room was a black piano. Its irresistible keys gave forth the most wonderful sounds: hollow bongs, mournful plinks and reverberating off-centre strums.

"It needs tuning," you said.

I nodded as if I knew what tuning was. If I had known I would not have agreed, as those untuned sounds were so weird and affecting.

The passageway walls bore two mirrors, one full length and seeming to confront one with an advancing stranger, the other, to which you lifted me, gorgeous with iridescent ladies and butterflies superimposed on the glass. I thought all mirrors should be like them and from then on found ours at home boring and featureless even when they framed my own features. I watched you as you gazed and dimpled at yourself. You were always at that mirror. You drew your fingers through your hair to the nape, and I wished mine were long, dark and loose too.

In the front room there was a black lacquer cabinet with scenes painted on it in red and gold. It contained pretty china ladies, some in crinolines, some in modern - that is 1920´s - dress.

"That's Josie," you pointed at one of the latter, "and that's the Doobarry - my very favourite one of all."

It seemed a funny name for a lady, but I could see she was special with her high-built hair, blue-dot eyes and pink bodice fitting into a billowing and garlanded skirt.

"Is your mamma like her?" I asked.

Your dimples grew very mobile as

"We-ell - sort of - p'raps," you replied.

When I did meet her I could see that Mrs Foster was not exactly like the Dubarry. But she was dainty. So why did she answer to two different names? Her mother and father, and most people, called her Carrie or Caroline. But your dad called her Cara, and this was the name she wanted the general public to know her by, even though Grom called it "a daft bloody name".

Cara was the woman she made sure men saw and fell for. She had long peroxided hair falling in Veronica Lake style, and a neat taut figure, clothed perfectly to show it off. She liked to stand with hand on hip, high bust pointing forward, knowing that men's eyes were on her. Butchers, bobbies, doctors, pot-bank managers, bus drivers, window cleaners and delivery boys hovered round her doorway like dogs, all but cocking up their legs to leave indications of interest. It was common knowledge that your dad, a long distance lorry driver, was often away from home.

Carrie's was the face turned to other women and us kids and, to tell the truth, it was somewhat hard. It had the dry wind-lined skin of her father's, but her hair hid most of it and the latest "Hollywood" cosmetics worked wonders. Actually, men didn't seem to mind about the hardness - the thrust of the bust and the flex of the buttocks drove them crazy. Most potent of all - a come-on apparently unknown to all the other women in the neighbourhood - was the way she carried herself, like a film star, with arrogantly lifted chin and straight shoulders squaring up to the gathered weight of her platinum hair and to other women's view of her.

The effect was superb and gave me a totally different concept of womanhood from any I had yet encountered. My mother and most women I knew were unselfish, droopy and long suffering, making the best of a bad job and snatching at small consolations. I was already in the process of becoming my mother's small consolation, the ear to which she confided her sorrows. When she confided them to your mother she was told not to be "such a bloody fool!" This was followed by an assurance that all men were "shitbags" and, therefore, to be treated "like dirt". By way of illustration Cara pressed a tiny pointed snakeskin-cased foot on the yard bricks and twisted her raised high heel.

"That's what my husband called me," Mamma said. "A shitbag - among other things."

It was true: I had heard him say it, and had felt it just as she had, worse than a blow. Now, hearing you mother's verdict on men, I felt reassured: if men and women generally saw each other as shitbags, my parents were not so peculiar after all. From that moment I became a double agent in the sex war, listening and watching and taking note.

"Then you should leave him. No woman should put up with that."

"What can't be cured must be endured."

"You should give as good as you get." Your mother spoke with the assurance of one who gave better than she got.

"Two wrongs don't make a right," was what my mother always said to such advice, which was often given.

"But you should never surrender. Give men an inch and they take an ell. Hark at me! I gave up show business to get married. Our M'reen's not going to make the same mistake. She's going on the stage if it's the last thing I do. She's not going to be at the mercy of any shitbag."

"But if she falls in love - I mean - " Mamma said with a hopeless abandon, "-you don't mind what men do to you if you love them."

"Love - pooph!" Cara's shoulders became squarer than ever.

It was a summer's day early in the war: the four of us you, I and our mothers were in the local park when suddenly from loudspeakers hidden in the lilac and rhododendron trees came dance music. Like tribeswomen at some predetermined ritual our mothers got up from the grass and danced, wound in each other's arms. You and I watched in surprised delight. Then, drawn into the spell, we danced too.

Dance was the essence of your life as it was of your mother's. When we flopped down on the grass for our picnic, I heard her telling Mamma how she had met your dad at a dance. But not as a partner. Sid Foster was the drummer in the band, in show business no less, and she watched him intently as he went through his routine, his head, glossed with brilliantine and sweat, going mad with the bash and whack on skin and shimmering metal. Then at the interval, having spotted her standing there, arms akimbo on her red satin hips, pistol-packing bust about to fire, he leapt off the platform and offered her a drink.

"Something exotic," he said, wiping his brow with a white handkerchief. "Just like you."

It was the sort of approach Carrie liked, but "Ey, Mac," came a harsh interruption from the gangly fellow she had come with.

She hoped there would be a fight over her, for Sid gave such an impression of manliness. He was thickset and bullish looking. Later, she found out that the round face and rounded body, the slicked back hair and big brown dago eyes, betokened the feminine within. He was large but loose muscled and, ultimately, after much bluster, yielding. But she did not see that then. Even if she had, her escort's next words settled the matter:

"Carrie's mine - get it, pal?"

Carrie's hands went back to her hips and she gave her shoulders a Mae West swagger:

"Oh, Carrie's yours, is she? Well, get this in your numbskull. The name's Cara, and Cara belongs to nobody. Cara pleases herself."

Later that night she let the drummer drive her home in his lorry, with the cymbals crashing behind them over the bumpy tracks. "Home" wasn't just the wrong side of them, it was way beyond anywhere. "Home" was a shack along the canal-side.

"Shack" was how Cara described it, but to me, when you and your granddad took me there, it was paradise. We went by barge, slowly passing the pot-banks whose yards came down to the water. We went smooth as pharaohs surveying our subjects and their labours. Here ware baskets were stacked, white and beige and brown, smelling of oriental marshes baked in sun. There was also the smell of evaporating turpentine that accompanied all work. Loose-singleted kilnsmen ambled in and out of their ovens, ablaze in blazing June, as if they were used to Hell and found it not so bad after all. They smoked their fags and gazed dreamily into the dense green water, then ambled back to stoke the fires which, for the pottery if not the people, were purgatorial: it would come out white and pristine, edged with gold and flowers and ready for far-off places, while they went home, dirty and tired and a day nearer doom. Beyond rose two slender chimney towers vying for supremacy over our little lives: Johnson's square and grey as of the medieval north, and Meakins's red and round like an Arabian minaret. Both sent the same yellow clouds, like impure prayers, into the blue sky, but the sky did not heed them. Neither did we as we floated out to the fields, and the chimneys became thin little sticks, like dying Roman Candles, on our retrospective horizon. The canal travelled indifferently through town or country, but Granddad was glad to be in the greenness and took loud sniffs of its juiced breath. I loved being within tugging distance of the growth that lined the towpath, but shed a few deliberate tears when I found I had tugged at nettles. You had to wipe my hand with burdock and then "kiss it better", and your kiss was softer than Dadda's and just as longed for.

Then there it was: the shack where your mother had grown into her impressive womanhood.. In its abandoned state it looked woebegone now, but I saw at once why Granddad preferred living in his daughter's lavatory to living in her house. The shack was like a luxury outdoor closet. It was made of old boat wood with faded paintings on it, unnameable flowers and upside-down primitive landscapes and odd bits of words " liffe", " veyo..", "Bros Lt " and " egd." The hut looked egged, on its platter of buttercups and cow parsley. There was a narrow veranda with a broken balustrade, and a rickety faded deckchair which Grandad sat on and, in pokerfaced fashion, made collapse under him. We collapsed too. Inside was all wood, grainy grey like the wood lice that trundled about. It was the next best thing to a boat, and the green lapping light of the canal came in at the windows.

Grom had always wanted to live on dry land and so the hut had been built for her. And then Carrie, who attended a proper school, started dreaming of a proper house in a proper street as other girls had. It was the only ordinary thing she did want. Her other dream was to be "in show business". Instead she married the drummer.

She soon searched out his weaknesses as surely as a boatee would find the untarred seams of his barge. On the other hand, Sid was the ideal husband for Cara, because he was an often absent one, thanks to the long distance driving.

Admirers were what Cara needed. She wanted to be idolised but not to be "messed about", for why should she surrender to wills inferior to her own? So, when she graciously consented to go out with an admirer, she always took somebody else along to rule out what she called "the funny business". Mostly it was you she took along with her. On one such occasion Mamma and I stood peeping through our front bedroom curtains to watch a two-seater car with a dicky draw up next door. A man jumped out, balding, middle-aged (your mother's escorts were mostly over forty and "in business"), and tapped lightly in a significant rhythm at the front window. Then she would emerge, wearing a gleaming silk scarf round her head and yanking your hand. The admirer tucked you into the dicky seat with a blanket and a bar of Fry's. Ceremoniously he opened the tiny passenger door, which your mother could have easily stepped over, and she settled herself way down so near the ground I thought they were going to move the vehicle by foot. But no, with a blast of exhaust, they zoomed off into the sunset. Then Mamma would tut-tut and I would sigh, both envying them in our different modes, she for the admirer and the drive, I for the drive and the Fry's.

One wonderful occasion I did travel in that dicky seat with you. The driver was called Victor, though he should have been called Vanquished since you mother had him at her mercy for months. On this occasion she also invited her friend, Rita Philpotts, to join the party. Rita was wild and wilful, with dark curly hair, flashing eyes and thickly carmined lips below a faint moustache. She loved to move her massive hips in what she called "Latin-American rhythm" and actually liked being known as Rio Rita, though your mother called this "common". While Cara occupied the passenger seat of the small car, Rita splayed herself generously across its back part. Whenever we peeped up from our place in the open boot we were confronted by the black satin split of her buttocks, and we laughed noiselessly. She had let one of her shoes drop between your mother and Victor and was now tantalisingly tickling Victor's ear with a stockinged toenail. Cara's built-up shoulders expressed irritation at finding a gross foot (Rita took size sevens) between herself and her fancy man. (She became even more irritable later, when Victor married Rita after what your mother liked referring to, in Rita's presence, as "a messy divorce").

It was a blissful day for me. This seemed the only possible way to travel, tucked up against you, now all I could possibly want in a life's companion. You were as protective and inventive as my father, but not moody and frightening as he had become. Just as we reached journey's end, there was a terrific thunderstorm. Victor carried us, wrapped in rugs, into the house. Me first. As he hugged me to his motoring togs, I noticed that he gave you a wink. His arms were strong and protective. I knew I was safe, even from the lightning that cracked the sky around us. Before he lifted me out of the boot, he carefully took his wet and half-smoked cigarette from his mouth, pinched the burnt end between his fingers, and pocketed it for future use, just as my father would have done. The smoke and nicotine lingered round his rain-damp chin, and it was like the smell of my father. It is strange how different tobacco smoke smells on men from the way it does on women, something to do with sweat or make-up or the different brands. Cara and Rita were addicted to Craven A: it permeated their perfume and the spirituous scalp-tingling scent of their varnished nails.

It took some time for Victor to fetch you in from the car, and your mother was strangely curt and suspicious-sounding when he finally breezed in with you, a large and leggy babe-in- arms. You gave me the smile that usually signified you had some secret to impart, but if you had, you never told me what it was.

"Would a pub lunch be in order?" As soon as he asked the question he regretted it. He wasn't sure he wanted to take Maureen out for a drive let alone into a pub. The nun nodded enthusiastically.

"Oh, we'd like that very much, wouldn't we, darling?"

"No."

"Ah, don't be like that. You know you'd love to go for a drive with your old friend - and a spot of lunch to follow. What could be nicer than that?" The nun turned to Jack. "Take no notice - she always says no when she means yes."

"So does she say yes when she means no?"

The nun sighed as she applied make-up to Maureen's blatantly yawning face.

"If it were only that simple. She says no all the time. They all say no to anything out of the routine. Now, let's see what we shall put on - something really smart. I know - your blue suit and a white blouse. Only I hope you won't make a mess of it as you did when - well -"

The suit and blouse were at last arranged on Maureen's uncooperative body.

"It's so good for them to get out and about in the real world. You'd be surprised what a difference it makes. There, doesn't she look as pretty as a picture?"

It seemed odd for a nun to be concerned about prettiness, even in other women, and Maureen was not pretty now, but powder blue was her colour, and the geriatrics' hairdresser had been in the day before, so she looked presentable if a little abstracted.

"Am I driving?" she enquired as the passenger door was opened for her.

"Not today, darling. Apparently - " the nun added as if in confidence, "she was an advanced driver in her day."

Maureen opened her handbag and produced a plastic wallet.

"Here's my license."

It was Australian, still apparently valid. Could such a skill remain despite dementia? Maureen seemed determined to show that it could - she dashed round to put herself in the driver's seat.

"Oh no, darling," the nun cried, rushing to extricate her. "Ladies don't drive when they have a charming male escort."

Jack winced and said,

"Your very own chauffeur."

At last, after much persuasion, tugging and redness of face, they got her into the passenger seat. As Jack started the car,

"Chauffeur!" Maureen scoffed, digging at his ribs. "Where's your cap then? Chauffeur!"

She went on murmuring the word as they were waved off, glancing round at him now and then as if wondering who the devil he was. She read aloud the number plates of the vehicles ahead and, when they stopped at lights, she read out the words on rear window stickers, including one that said, "You don't have to be mad to be a passenger in this car but it helps." As she mouthed the words like a child showing how well it could read, they seemed to apply to Jack's car rather than the one in front.

They could have driven straight out into the country, but he had already decided he should take her past their old haunts, to see if some submerged memories might be dredged up. He steeled himself to drive through the self-styled city, displaced and disorientated by one-way systems and extravagant by-passes, a ruin of what it was and a poor imitation of what it strove to be. In fact - he might have guessed - most of their childhood scene had disappeared. As the Potteries no longer made pottery, there were no warehouses, no bottle ovens, no boats on the cut, only attempts at urban renewal for people who had no particular reason to be in that no longer viable urban place.

His heart outpaced the car-revs as he drove along their street, past the once-continuous terraces, now gaping with parking lots, half the houses bricked up and the other half given over to what Graham Greatbatch had called "immigrants and students and that sort of thing".

"Look!" he cried, jauntily, pointing. "There's where we used to live. And there's Lidgetts' and Hands' - and isn't that Aggie's place?"

"Aggie who's?" Maureen scanned and saw nothing of what he

saw. And since all the people whose names he was giving to the houses had long gone, she was seeing the reality, he only a dream.

He had planned to stop and walk her round to the back alleyways, the gates and yards and outdoor loos which, far more than streets and front doors, had formed the heart of their world. But he could see there was no point, no recognition, no shared feeling. He was alone in the pain of memory. Besides, the alleys had lost their cobbles and were now blocked by clapped out cars. In helpless anger he asked a direct question, just what the nun had warned him not to do.

"Don't you remember anything? Don't you even remember Graham Greatbatch?"

"You mean that big lad as lives by the builder's yard?"

Jack's heart skipped. Had he at last found the key to the lost mansions of her mind?

"So you remember Molds?"

"Moles?"

"Molds. Don't you remember the lavatory?"

"Yes." He almost gave a hooray, but , "You can take me there right now."

"Take you to Molds?"

"The lav, you stupid bugger. I'm dying for a jimmy riddle."

She gazed around smiling, as if at an audience who should applaud her triumph and his discomfiture. That phrase, he recalled," a jimmy riddle" was the one his father used and used all the more when the young Maureen had gleefully laughed at it.

Fearing pollution of his car, he drove like mad along the city's longest artery and out into the country. By the time they reached their destination, however, Maureen seemed to have forgotten her jimmy riddle. The pub could have been anywhere from the Home Counties to Cumbria, offering "home made traditional food" and "a friendly atmosphere", its yard full of the posh cars of the retired who were now guzzling their way through the pensioners' menu. He hated to admit that he was one of them, looking, with Maureen on his arm, every bit as married as they did.

"Would you like a glass of Australian wine?" he asked her when they had found an empty table, next to a large party of what looked like former teachers. One of their numbers had them in fits and they were as rowdy as delinquent children.

Maureen shook her head.

"Bird," she replied.

"No, I mean to drink. But does that mean you'd prefer chicken to fish?"

"Bi-ird," she chortled, mimicking drinking.

"Bird?"

She nodded happily.

His heart raced. That had been her favourite drink when she was eleven.

"Dandelion and Burdock! Is that what you want?'

'Go on!' She laughed.

When he got his turn at the bar, he asked in his most unctuous and confidential tones,

"Do you - er -by any chance - er - still stock - er- Dandelion and Burdock?"

"You what, duck?"

"Dandelion and Burdock." He shrank into himself, hoping nobody else had heard the request.

"I'll have to ask the manager about that."

The bar-tender consulted her employer who laughed.

"He said we haven't done that in donkey's years."

"Diet Coke's the nearest thing," the manager shouted from the end of the bar and was heard murmuring "Dandelion and Burdock" and laughing with his "regulars".

So Diet Coke it had to be, though when she put it to her lips, Maureen didn't seem to mind. But neither did it kindle any remembrance.

He didn't ask her what she wanted to eat but ordered fish and chips as the nun had directed.

When the food came he couldn't understand why she systematically worked through the chips down to the last one and then sat smilingly contemplating the still whole fish. It took him some time to realise that she needed to have it cut up into bite-size pieces.

Mercifully, the teachers were too bound up in themselves to notice. Their hubbub masked the silence at the next table. However, once Maureen's hands were free of dealing with food, they found their way to her skirt, which she began peeling carefully back from her knees, hem length by hem length. He was aghast. He dared not be seen by the public to put his hand to her thighs. The teachers' discomfort began to be palpable as more and more thigh was revealed. So

"D'you want to visit the toilet?" he whispered.

"No."

No could mean yes, he told himself. "I'll take you."

He lifted her almost bodily, hoping the skirt would fall into place and he could have his pee while she had hers. Only one side of the skirt dropped, while the other exposed her undies. And, as luck would have it, the "Ladies" and "Gents" were at opposite ends of the bar, so he was witnessed pushing the woman through the Ladies' door and then hovering foolishly, wondering whether he dared leave her to her own devices. As gents usually perform more quickly than ladies, he decided to risk attending to his own needs. He emerged from the urinal to see Maureen, her skirt still awry around her thighs, making her way back to the table. Only, it was the wrong table. She homed in on a chair that had just been vacated by the life and soul of the teacher's party. The teachers were suddenly very quiet, squirming under Maureen's fixed gaze like a quelled class and trying to avoid looking at her nearly visible crotch. She reached for the nearest glass, took a swig, then gave a theatrical grimace and belch. The former occupant of the chair returned, cooing,

"There was this funny old woman in the - " She broke off, finding the funny old woman in her place.

"Arseholes!" was Maureen's response to polite urgings that she should move to her own place.

Creased up, Jack intervened with,

"I'm sorry - so sorry. She's not dangerous, just confused, that's all."

He tried to raise her but she would not budge. She looked up at him.

"How the bloody 'ell did you get in here?" she asked. "You crafty sod!"

The other customers now looked at him in silence as if waiting for an answer to the same question. In fact they were all wondering, as he was himself, how he would get her out of there. He tried raising her again, but she set up the kind of yowl that only a nun could cope with. Then he had what he called later "a brainwave".

"Your chauffeur awaits you," he announced. Mercifully, nobody laughed.

She smiled and slowly stood up and, with her skirt hem still somewhere round her hips, let him lead her out.

It was only when he had got her and himself safely tucked within the seatbelts of the car that he remembered that he had not paid the lunch bill. He had a vision of himself offering unctuous apologies

Maureen: After and Before

and explanations, something he felt he had spent his life doing. To hell with it! If Maureen could enjoy her second childhood, why should not he? He turned the key in the ignition and made the tyres screech and burn, as he had never done before, in their exit from the car park.

"Wouldn't it be nice to stop for a drink?" she asked gaily as they re-entered the city. "It's ages since I was last in a pub."

Maureen: After and *Before*

Graham Greatbatch was a large lovable boy, brown and soft as a teddy-bear, with button eyes and dark head-hugging hair. Even at age eight he had the slight shadow of a moustache. What I most liked about him was his comfortable dog smell and his large paw-like hands. He had large parents who also smelt of dog.

Their house was built on a scale to take servants. A glass-fronted box high on the kitchen wall contained different bells for summoning skivvies who no longer came. Old Holmes, Mr Greatbatch's employer, had built the place to his own specification, he being a builder and his yard being next door. Then the usual thing happened. Prospering, old Holmes was persuaded by his wife that they should move away from the "works". So Mr Greatbatch, the yard superintendent, moved in: the front, with its bay windows, became offices, and the back parts became the Greatbatches' living quarters. Old Holmes hovered in the background with his moustaches and wing collar, the elder son presided with his Homburg and watch-chain, and the surveyor surveyed through his pince-nez. The trilbied younger son occasionally dashed in for pocket money, legging from his sports car. There was also a clerk, Mr Reynolds, who looked like Anthony Eden and smoked a pipe of the sweetest smelling tobacco. The office smelt deliciously of this and also of "plans" which appeared on thick rolled parchment or crisp tracing paper. Then there was the smell of freshly sharpened pencils, Indian ink and Mrs Greatbatch when she had been in to dust.

The yard next door was full of bricks and wood and was surrounded by a high wall with broken glass embedded in its parapet. I had privileged passage into this world of work, and I loved the scent of the clean new planks weathering and oozing resin into the smoky air.

Instead of just stairs such as we had, the Greatbatch house had a proper staircase with banister, its handrail curving beautifully round the bottom pedestal. The landing was lit, or gloomed rather, by a leaded lancet window of yellow and purple glass which made melancholy pools on the linoleum and aroused unfathomable feelings in me. The bedrooms were gigantic and cavernous, smelling of mothballs and beer-piss, and there were giant size boscage-patterned chamber pots under the beds.

The bathroom was the very first I ever entered. It, too, was made for giants, with a long deep bath whose brass taps were beyond my little hands to turn. They dripped green lines down the white enamel, which felt like a salt block when one drew one's fingers across it. There was that damp cobwebby cockroachy odour of drains. Alongside the giants' hand basin stood, higher than me, the giants' lavatory pan. My feet dangled way above the floor when I sat on the dark crimson seat with its fine brass hinges, so different from the detachable deal wood seat at home. I had to be lifted on and off by the ever helpful Graham. I was like Gulliver in Brobdingnag, caressed and cherished by huge hands. When Graham inducted me into sex, my member in his hand was like the first tentative shoot from a hyacinth bulb. His in mine was a half-cooked sausage bursting through its skin.

All life with Graham was implicitly, or more often explicitly, sexual, and I raced randily home from the Infants' School to await his arrival from the Juniors. We would barricade ourselves in his father's shed to fondle one another as we observed the habits of the rabbits hutched there. The scent of straw and sawdust in the darkness brings back to me those dry orgasms. On winter evenings we would play with Graham's Dinky cars on the hearth while the senior Greatbatches sat at either side of the glowing range, like slumped colossi, working their way through a crate of ale. Prince, a cocker spaniel, twitched and whimpered in his dreams and was soothed by the female colossus. There was also a budgerigar called Dicky who knew his own name and address, and spent much of his time cursing Hitler in a ghostly echo of Mrs Greatbatch's voice.

When Mr Greatbatch did his paperwork and wore rimless half-glasses on his huge fat face, Graham and I would creep under the table he sat at. Mr Greatbatch could only sit with his massive thighs splayed wide apart. And because his fly buttons had long ago flown, and because he wore no underpants, his testicles, ragged like poppies bursting from their pods, were available for our inspection. Graham pointed out the varicosities of the scrotum. The overwhelming temptation to touch the object with the point of a pencil had to be resisted, but Prince showed no such restraint and came sniffing and licking, wagging his tail and smiling like the goof he was. At which Mr G's thighs would squeeze together and the balls would withdraw slowly into the trousers like eggs being taken under the breast of a brooding bird.

Even then I thought it strange that Graham could be so objective about his own father, and especially about his own father's balls. I would have died rather than seen my father in this way. But there was a reason. Graham was an adopted child. He vouchsafed this information to me one day as proof positive that babies weren't born by what we called "ooing" and via their mothers' fannies which we didn't believe any way. Graham produced his adoption papers, and I envied him: my own entry into the world lacked this clean official stamp.

I was not quite as obsessed with sex as Graham was, but perhaps because I was too small to have any of my own, I entered readily into other people's enthusiasms. And I was a born go-between. As, for example, between you and Graham. He said he needed to see a girl naked and did I know of one who would oblige? I said I was sure Maureen Foster would and arranged a meeting. Molds' house had been empty for years and the outdoor lavatory was going to rack and ruin. It could only be reached by climbing over the back gate whose lock was mysteriously renewed from time to time. Graham popped me over, leaving you to cope on your own. It was a hot day but we didn't take all our clothes off, only the bottom half needing to be exposed. The lavatory was being reclaimed by nature. Loosestrife and willow herb splayed out of the walls and the roof slates were held together by lichen. There was a strange smell, not of "cack" as you called it, screwing up your nose, but of general decomposition: the bricks were like old Dundee cake, the long brown pipe was being eaten away from below by earth and ancient sewage, the ducket had long ago stopped ducketing and was filled with fascinating and unspeakable matter. For all we knew the dimly-remembered Molds were mouldering away down there. But somehow the workings of nature made what we were about to attempt seem proper.

"Attempt" was the word, certainly on my part. I put my inadequate spout to your pink slit and jigged about in the way Graham recommended. He said this was what grownups did. He always seemed to know about their secret behaviour, having spent a lot of time spying on his parents in their sozzled semi-consciousness. The tightness of your slit was proof positive that babies could not possibly come that way.

For me the most memorable feature of the experience was the place where it happened, and the weather, the bright heat outside, the cool spidery shadows around us, the bee-busy flowers, the long nettles and the geometrical bits of blue sky where tiles had fallen away. The experience in itself was as minimal as I was, though we all pretended it had been a revelation.

It must have been about this time that I began to notice that the way people looked affected my feelings about them, and that there was a distinction to be made between feelings of affection and those of arousal. It even became important to discriminate between people one slept with. Hitherto, it hadn't mattered where, when or with whom one did it. It was when I went away on my first ever holiday that it became crucial.

The Greatbatches decided to take me with them on their annual trip to a niece's near Congleton. Mrs G. brought a small attaché case for my change of clothes: pyjamas, underwear, clean blouse and shorts and, my latest acquisition, a translucent green toothbrush. Mr Reynolds was to take us in his Morris. I had not been in a car before. Mr Reynolds stood twinklingly contemplating my excitement through his pipe smoke that smelt like a mixture of boiled-over jam and burnt roses. His straight-cut features and neat moustache gave me strange pleasure. It was not just his looks and his tobacco aroma. He represented a world I was destined to fall in love with: the world of gentility, in which everybody was nice to each other, didn't swear or break wind or smell other than sweet, and had homes filled with Axminister carpets and Westminster chimes.

It was hard to believe that Mr Reynolds and the Greatbatches were of the same species. Their antics made him give his crinkly smile and rearrange his pipe between his teeth. But if the Greatbatches were Neanderthals, they were Neanderthals full of love. It was love, not vanity that made Mrs G's packing so longwinded and comprehensive. Whilst Prince and Dicky were to come with us, she made Mr Reynolds swear on the Bible that he would tend to the welfare of the creatures left behind. Then she went to the shed to inform them of, and apologize for, the arrangement.

After debates and arguments and dashing in and out of the house, Mrs G., Graham and I were settling in the back of the Morris with Prince on Graham's knee and Dicky in his cage on Mrs G.'s. She was wearing a feathered hat which unnerved the bird and he fluttered all over his cage. I saw the beat of his heart where the feathers divided white on his breast.

"Dunna fret, Dicky, ducky," Mrs G. kept murmuring. "Mamma's with you and Dadda's coming too."

Graham smirked bitterly round at me. He didn't like to think of animals and birds as sharing parentage with him. I was waving to my family who stood at the kerbside with other folk from our street. At last Mr Reynolds and Mr G. were getting into their front seats. As the Neanderthal lowered his tremendous shanks we felt the Morris sink and groan. Mr Reynolds had had the foresight to place the couple diagonally to each other so that there was a balance. Mr Reynolds started the engine and Mrs G. gave a squawk.

"Where's me 'andbag? It's got me spare set in it."

Mr Reynolds stopped the car. Mr G. heaved out, muttering "Bloody fool!" and went back into the house. He emerged spreading his hands and saying

"Can't see the sodding thing anywhere."

"Ooh, men! Here, shug, fang 'olt o' this."

Mrs G. plonked the cage on me and wheezed her way out of the car. As she went Graham heaved a sigh and waved his hand between his nose and her disappearing behind.

"Poophh!" he breathed. "We'd be better off without her."

It seemed more shocking to be objective about one's mother than about one's father, even if she did stink. It was then that we saw the handbag squashed. It had been under Mrs G.'s behind all the time. Graham held it up as if it were something contaminated.

"You silly bugger," Mr G. said when his wife came out of the house wringing her hands. "You were sitting on it all along."

He glanced at Mr Reynolds, heaved a giant sigh and shook his head. Mr Reynolds twinkled and adjusted his pipe. Mrs G. opened the bag to make sure her spare teeth were still there. It was a large metal-framed handbag with a snapping clasp of knobbly silver, and only a behind like Mrs G.'s could have sat on it without knowing. It was a relief to me that, in spite of the teeth, the womanly smell of face powder wafted from the bag's inside. By now the spectators wanted to see the back of us. Mrs G's face had resumed its usual beaming vacancy. Graham was smirking ever more bitterly and trying to look as though he had nothing whatever to do with the scene. Dicky gazed at everything with eyes even more sardonic than Graham's. At last we were on our way in the hot sunshine, and I realised what Graham had meant about being better off without his mother.

The Greatbatch relations were as gigantic as they were, and it turned out that Graham had a huge amiable nine-year-old cousin called Norma. She and her parents lived on a small farm, a milky, uddery, cowpat-splattered, buttercup-spangled world. That evening I had milk expressed into a glass straight from the udder itself - so sweet and warm and different from any milk I could remember, since I could not remember my mother's. The cow shifted about heavily and gently, breathed likewise and peered round with chewing profile and bulging eye. Outside, the fields cooled and lengthened towards the sunset and Wales; eastwards hovered the blue drift of the Peak. Trees were dark and full-leafed. There were those scents of summer evening that take adults back to their childhood and children back to a time before memory. The virgin sky of wartime shone as it awaited violation.

Indoors, in the strawberry glow of a Welsh burner, I became conscious that the grown-ups were all looking gravely at me and urgently discussing something. I flushed and averted my head but kept my eyes slanting in their direction. What they were discussing was where I was to sleep. I had been an afterthought, not expected by the relatives. For a moment I felt alien and unwanted. Then the matter was settled and everybody relaxed. I was like the dog or the budgerigar, portable, dependent, putting myself wherever and into whatever position I was told to. So it had been up to that point. But within twenty-four hours I had a will of my own.

What had been decided was that I should sleep with Mr and Mrs Greatbatch. I did not fancy this arrangement. Mrs G. got me ready with a quick wipe of my hands and face from a brackish flannel. I insisted on cleaning my teeth with my new brush dipped into a splinter of cooking salt. Mrs G. and her niece took me upstairs and into the "best" bedroom, which was large, cold and musty from disuse. There stood a great bed of matrimony, all black bars and brass knobs, a bed that I should not fall out of, my head fitting neatly on the bolster and between two pillows that rose fatly on either side. There was a debate about whether the window should be open or not. I smelt the hay-smothered air and sneezed, so it was shut.

"Don't draw the curtains," I pleaded. "I want to see the light."

"Now goo sleep, pet," Mrs G. hushed. "Us'll be up presently."

The women tiptoed out as if I were already asleep. I heard their clatter on the stairs and their exclamations about how much the men had drunk in their absence. Then the kitchen door was shut and I heard the family only when they laughed, as they did increasingly. I heard the cries of owls rousing for their night-shift and I cried too, for my dadda and mamma, wishing I could hear the clunk of shunting engines, the whirr of pit-wheels and the hum of the Potteries kilns. It was still light, the infinite twilight of war-time summer. Time stretched and spread around me without horizon. The windowed sky showed space vacant and untouchable. The straw mattress shifted spikily under me. Wherever I ventured a toe I touched the cold starched wastes of the sheet. Claws scuttled in the loft and eaves, making me hunch my head into my shoulders under the bedclothes.

But something was urging me to leave my snowy plateau and tiptoe over the lino to the window casement. There I saw the farmyard in its diagonal shadows and the fields fading from green to grey. In the sky stood one sharp star, near to the even sharper new moon. Mamma used to say it was bad luck to see the new moon through glass. I felt bereft, an orphan, my family miles away, unreachable, going to their beds, forgetful of my existence. Tides of self-pity overtook me and washed me far out. I scrambled back to the uncomforting bed and sobbed myself to sleep.

I was awakened by the colossi heaving their sodden bulks upstairs. Prince came in first, snuffling and sliding on the lino. Peeping over the sheet I watched a hand carrying a candle appear waveringly round the door. Mr G. lurched and stumbled about the landing.

"Hush up, you clumsy bugger," said his wife, "else you'll wake John Willy here."

"Is there a jerry in that cupboard?" the man slurred.

Mrs G. and Prince went to look.

"Here y'are - dunna drop it."

It took Mr G. ages to relieve himself. He gasped and sighed and said,

"Eeh, that's better," and then "Blast!" when his aim went haywire with a rat-tat-tat on the lino.

"For God's sake, you dirty swine!" his wife hissed.

Then she took the pot and I heard a broad gush. My heart sank as the time came near when they would be getting into bed with me. It wasn't quite as near as I supposed. Mr G. removed his collar and trousers and stood swaying in his shirt. He opened the window wide and took deep draughts of the night air. Then he stood with his hands on the sill, whistling tunelessly at the moon.

"Eeh, but it's champion here, i'n't it?"

"It's lovely," his wife agreed, adding warily, "in the summer-time." She gave a terrific belch. "That's better. I've been dying get rid of it all night."

She did not come to bed till she had got rid of a barrage of wind. Meanwhile Mr G. took a few more draughts of night air, then closed the window softly. Simultaneously the giants got into bed on either side of me. Though drunk they were very careful and gentle. Mr G. lay on his back and his great breaths soon became juddering snores. Mrs G. stayed sitting up while she freed her hair of many pins that tinkled into a dish. I kept my thumb in my mouth, feigning sleep. Peeping over my knuckles, I could see in the candle-light something I had never seen before: Mrs G's hair hanging squaw-like round her flabby shoulders and arms. Then arms and hair wound me in an embrace. As the night wore on, the Greatbatches seemed to get larger, and I smaller. Nor was Prince, normally my soft spaniel buddy, any comfort now. First he explored the strange room, slithering and snuffling in every corner. He whimpered at the contrariness of human beings who weren't satisfied with the comfort of their own home. Then he jumped on the bed and, having sniffed at our faces, turned round and round in quest of the perfect position and found it at last in the lower part of the groove between Mr and Mrs Greatbatch. As I occupied the upper part of it, this meant that I was trapped in all directions.

Small wonder that when I dozed off I had one of my smothering nightmares. In their sleep the colossi spoke, in voices like those of Frankenstein's monster and his bride. I screamed. Prince leapt up and barked. Mr G. started awake with a snort.

"What the bloody 'ell's that?"

"Oh God in Heaven! Was it the air-raid warning or a cock crowing?"

"I think it was the little un."

"Oh, the mite - whatever's the matter, me darling?"

How could I tell her that she and her husband were the matter, how do other than let her draw me to her Brobdingnagian bosom, while her loose smoky hair stranded across my mouth and eyes?

Next day, after breakfast of salty rolled oats and buttered egg - real egg, not re-constituted - we children went out to play in the paradise of sheds, cotes and barns. Graham proposed our favourite game and Norma joined zestfully in, displaying what she hadn't got and examining what we had.

However, Graham did not suggest doing what we had done with you, dear Maureen. This was because, as he explained to me later in the strictest confidence, people went funny if they had relations with their relations. So he had heard his mother say. The day and our doings in it were so engrossing that I forgot the night before, and, more crucially, the night ahead.

But when suppertime came and the long twilight before the lamp was lit, the Greatbatches suddenly noticed that I was missing. Whilst eating my ham sandwich I was overwhelmed with homesickness and such a longing for my mother's turpentine-scented jumper that I slid down under the massive oak dining table to hide and cry behind the fringe of its heavy cloth. Prince came and joined me joyfully, and I anchored myself round his neck. A strong smell came from above us of ale and very rindy clothbound cheese, with the prickle of peppercorned pickles. I scrabbled at the rag rug to get at the bald hessian just as I did at home. It was small comfort. Time had caught up with me, or I had caught up with time, as I realised that another terrible night was in view. Two heads appeared upside down at the chenille fringe.

"He's here," Graham said through his upside down lips.

"What is it, duckie?" called Mrs G. "Have you got belly ache? It'll be them pickles, mark my words."

"It isn't the pickles," I called back in a still small voice.

"He's tired, that's what it'll be," said Norma's dad. "He's had too much fresh air. You folk from the Potteries aren't used to it."

I watched the man's legs uncross themselves and his toes clench in the old shoes that served as slippers. The faces disappeared, and there were only legs now, twelve of them, like a paling.

"I'm not tired," that voice spoke again, almost independently of me. "I want to go home. I want my mamma."

"I thought as much," said Norma's mamma.

"Ooh ducky," cried Mrs G. "You conna goo wom yet. The 'oliday's only just begun. Mr Reynolds'll be fetching us back Sat'dey. It wunna be long t'wait."

There was a pause while I counted on my fingers the number of nights till Saturday. Then I started to wail. Prince whined and licked my face.

"Never mind, pet, never mind." Mrs G. called. "Dunna fret thysen. We'll phone Mr Reynolds in the morning and see if he can fetch us before Sat'dey." She then lowered her voice, but I still heard. "Eeh, it's a bit of a bugger, i'n't it."

Seeing that I got instant attention by crying, I did it some more. But this time Norma's mother snapped,

"Less of thy blarting, young fellow-me-lad. You're a big boy now, you know, and big boys don't cry for their mammas."

"But I'm still little," came that voice again, a voice I hardly recognised as my own, it was so sharp and certain.

There was laughter at this, especially from Norma's dad.

"That's telling you," he said.

"Well, tomorra we'll see about takkin' you wom," promised Mrs G. "Now come on out and let me carry you upstairs to bed."

Several tentacles extended under the table, but I cringed out of reach.

"Whatever'll we do? We conna leave him under the table all night."

"We couldna 'ave a drink in peace."

Norma's right-way-up face suddenly appeared next to mine.

"Come on, duck," she whispered. "Tell me what's the matter."

At last, after some lovely cuddling and kissing away of my tears, I whispered in her ear.

"D'you know what?" she announced blatantly to the elders above. "He hates sleeping with Auntie Dolly and Uncle Perce."

I writhed in shame and remorse, especially at the way this was put. I hadn't actually used the word "hate" and I felt betrayed. Whatever were people going to think of me now? It was bad enough to spoil the holiday, but to insult my benefactors was unforgivable. I tried to make myself so small that I might disappear altogether and thus solve all our problems. But even after much effortful shrinking I was still intractably there. How was I to face the world beyond the chenille tablecloth ever again, how leave the companionable rag rug and the darkness?

There was an urgent low-voiced consultation over the crates. Norma smoothed my hair away from my forehead and by degrees coaxed, pushed and dragged me into the moth-mobbed strawberry light. There I was exposed to all gazes, my bad inner thoughts made public and subject to debate. Even Dicky stared at me from his cage, his little eyes full of disapproval.

"There's nowt for it," said Norma's mam, "he'll have to sleep with 'er and 'im."

"As I said in the first place," her husband sniffed.

"But it's only a single bed and those two're too big for it any way. Besides, it's not decent as it is."

"But he's only a little titch."

I was puzzled about the indecency, but my heart leapt with new joy as I realised, from the direction of the glances, that I was going to sleep with Norma and Graham.

"He's Tom Thumb, that's who he is," said Mr Greatbach, sweeping me on to his knee. I dared not look into his eyes and kept myself taut and averted.

I couldn't believe it: not only had they forgiven me for being so awful, but they were actually changing their arrangements to suit me. I was no longer a small pet object to be disposed of as others saw fit: I had a will of my own, preferences to express. And Mr G. was stroking my forehead as if it weren't the most terrible thing in the world to be told that somebody hated sleeping with you.

It was all agreed. Norma's bed-room had a ceiling that sloped down towards the windows. It was jolly and cosy with dolls and comics and the first vanities of girlhood: hair slides, ready made bows, mother's old make-up jars, and toffees saved for a rainy day or night. Norma gave me a liquorice allsort covered in tiny grains of turquoise sugar. It oozed through my tooth-gaps and down my tear-salted chin. Norma got a wet flannel and cleaned me up, then changed me into my pyjamas as she would have done a doll. From the moment I had whispered my secret in her ear, and even though she had so vulgarly broadcast it to the world, I was crazy about her and dimly aware that this was not only because she was nice natured, but she was nice looking as well. Just at that moment, dear Maureen, I even preferred her to you!

The bed was arranged in a most interesting manner because Norma and Graham were, as Norma's man put it, "of the opposite sex". They, therefore, slept upside down to one another, one's feet to the other's head. My length being about the width of the bed, I was placed laterally, my head by Norma's and my feet by Graham's.

It was blissful having my nose in Norma's hair and tangling my toes with Graham's. Norma kept asking "Can I do you now, sir?" while Graham sang "This old man, this old man, he played three, he played knickknack on my knee," until Norma's mother put her head in at the door and said,

"Now that's quite enough of that. Little Jacky needs his sleep. I shall put him back with Auntie Dolly and Uncle Perce if you carry on like this."

At which I gave a big "Shush!" to my companion. I didn't in fact get much of the needed sleep. In the quietness I heard first Graham's and then Norma's breathings get longer and deeper as they left me on the shore of wakefulness. I felt an overwhelming grief at the thought of how far away my mamma and dadda were, and how lucky Norma and Graham were to have theirs with them under the same roof.

The new day opened up a new world and even if it only existed and lasted for a day, it affected my whole lifetime. We (all except Dicky, that is) took a ride in the milk cart towards the hills. It was not like the pony and trap that brought our milk at home, but a great flat dray with a large horse whose buttocks were more impressive even than Mr Greatbatch's. It looked at us darkly from behind its blinkers. Mrs.G expressed concern about its having to pull such a weight of humanity.

"Dunna fret," the driver scoffed. "This oss'll tak' a baker's dozen o'churns and not flinch, and they're 'eavier than us."

This didn't seem likely to me, and I was relieved that, whenever there was uphill work, we got off and walked. Slowly, very slowly, the hills drew near, changing from a soft blue haze to a solid bulwark of heather, red rock and bilberry bushes. I had never been so close to what I called a mountain before, and its name, as whispered by Norma, was the first poetry I learned after nursery rhymes and carols: Cloud End. Cloud End, I repeated over and over, and on that day the edge of that escarpment with its silver cloud-quiff became the archetype of all later hills.

"Dost want goo up top?" asked Norma's dad, his large face with its shiny red nose and red cheeks beaming down at me like Mr. Punch's.

"Ooh no fear, Wilfy," Mrs G. replied.

"I didna meyn thee, Dolly, I meant Tom Thumb here."

"Ey now, dunna overtax him. He's only a tiddler."

"But he's a lad, inner 'e?"

"And I'm a girl," Norma declared fiercely. "And I'm going up. Come on, Gray."

She and Graham set off on the track through the young heather. I followed as manfully as my unmanly legs allowed.

Norma's dad brought up the rear, leaving the others behind in the cart, where they passed each other the binoculars to look at Cheshire. I had not gone far before I drooped, and Norma's dad lifted me on to his shoulders, holding my legs round his neck. The sense of the strong shoulders and the steadying grip was as thrilling to me as the mountain itself. I gazed down at his head which, like the mountain, had a bald red patch at the top but, unlike the mountain, no white cloud to hide it. Every time I looked at the patch, I longed to touch it as I would have touched my father's. To take my mind off the bald patch I surveyed the landscape, my head swivelling this way and that. I was level with the tops of birches and rowans and looked down on sheep hidden amongst bracken. I snatched at moths shimmering up from the heather at the giant's tread.

As we neared the summit I reached up and touched the sky. And then the man turned, ever so slowly, carefully turning me with him. There was the great plain with its grouped trees, misting to distance. Somewhere, along the line of the man's pointing finger, was his farmhouse, and it seemed impossible that the world was at once so vast and so small, bigger than mountains and men, smaller than me. I felt hollow inside, and the sudden yearning for home flooded over me again like music. I was afraid of all this space and freedom. I longed for limits and the pastry smell of my mother's pinafore.

"Put me down," I commanded, and miraculously the man obeyed. Up to then grownups had always seemed to please themselves, not me.

Charged with energy I began hurtling downhill, desperate to escape from this freedom and air. I knew it was glorious but I could not bear it. I ran and ran, stumbling, falling, sliding on my trouser-seat, picking myself up, hearing warning voices but wanting only to get down, down, away from the future that had called to me on that height. The path ended at a narrow stile in the wall, and there was the road and the milk cart with its three large adults sitting watching me curiously as if watching a sequence in a film which they could do nothing about. I did not see individual things through my sweat, only an undifferentiated mass which, though bigger than my own body, seemed much smaller than the world of fears and longings that I contained.

Nor did I see the danger I was in. I was either going to go smack into the wall or, if I plunged over the stile, straight on to the road. But a strong arm caught me just as I reached it. Norma's dad held me up as if I were no more than a rabbit whose neck he was about to snap. I struggled in the power of the big hands and didn't know whether to feel safe or scared. The man's face looked both angry and tender. I gave myself up to the giant's arms, and the world became itself again.

Norma and Graham were haring down the path, eager to see what had happened.

"That settles it," I heard Mrs G. say. "We shall have tak' him wom. He's too much of a handful."

"Well," winked Norma's dad. "For a little un tha mak'st a big splash in the pond."

"It'd be the best thing," his wife added and nudged her aunt. "you can always come back without him."

I flushed, angry at the thought that they would ditch me, and then everything would go on in my absence.

"I'd never forgive mesen," said Mrs G. "if he came t'any 'arm."

Graham and Norma were looking gravely at each other, anticipating premature separation. They then looked at me accusingly. I felt terrible. Yet I also felt a strange triumph in that I seemed to have become so important.

The day was not over, however. We still had our food to eat, and Norma's dad drove the dray to their favourite picnic spot. It was up an avenue of overgrown rhododendrons and on to wild moorland above. Here was heather, and rock again, and we were, though I didn't know it, on Cloud End's other side. A number of huge stones stood, some flat, some upright, like the work of giants who could have been ancestors of those I was with. In the shelter of the stones Norma's mother spread out cloths and emptied baskets for a feast that in war-time only farmers could put on: cheese, ham, hardboiled eggs, scones with jam and cream, milk for me and tea for everybody else. Our exploits had made us hungry and I tucked in, causing smiling glances to pass between the elders.

"You'd think he'd look like Primo Carnera the way he eats," said Norma's dad.

"What he needs is some 'ossmuck in his shoes," said Mrs Greatbach, "That'd make him grow."

"There's plenty of that on our farm," said Norma's mamma. "We shall have to see what we can do about it."

I hated this talk and even more the laughter which greeted it.

"I'd rather stay small," I muttered.

The wasps buzzed about us and the grasshoppers whirred their legs beneath ours. Soft breezes breathed through the magenta dots of heather. Something about the place, or maybe just our concentration on eating, made us fall silent - well, not silent but speechless: as always with the Greatbatches there was much lip-smacking, tea-slurping and, when satiety set in, ritual belching. Mrs G. went through her routine of fingering tasty titbits round her mouth and then splatting them out for Prince to pounce on. The elders yawned and began to nod off, stretching themselves on the red-glinting moorland grass. They looked like the giants of the megaliths put to sleep by magic. The sunlit shires lay in their haze, happy with summer and heedless of war. Graham put a finger to his lips and beckoned Norma and me to follow him outside of the stone enclosure. Looking back at the large loose sleepers who were like grounded barrage balloons under the endangered sky, Norma was reminded of something - something, it seemed, she had been dying to ask.

"What did it feel like - " her thumb indicated the two greater Greatbatches " - sleeping with them?"

I glanced at Graham, not wanting to be too brutal in front of their, albeit adopted, son. I need not have scrupled, however, for

"Putrid," he answered for me, pinching his nose with one hand and making a chain-pulling gesture with the other. "I should know - I've had a basinful."

"It was," I nodded in sober agreement, "putrid," our favourite word just then.

"Did they do anythink?"

"How d'you mean?"

"You know - anythink?" Norma winked at her cousin.

"Don't you mean any thing?" I asked, gonging the "g".

"Well, anything then," Norma assented in a subdued tone.

I shrugged.

"They belched and trumped and that, and Graham's dad got up from time to time to piddle in the jerry and - "

"Missed his aim," Graham put in. "If I know him."

"Is that all?" Norma seemed disappointed.

"What else would they do asleep?"

"Get us."

"Get us?"

"It's what me mam says. She says babies come when parents are asleep. They have a dream together and it turns out to be us."

"They have to oo as well." Graham observed urbanely.

"Like we did with Maureen," I blabbed.

"Who's Maureen?" Norma's voice suddenly sounded harsh and strange.

"Just some tart or other." Graham spoke as if it hardly needed saying.

"I only wondered," Norma said, obviously still wondering.

"Wondered what?"

"Whether Auntie Dolly and Uncle Percy did it."

"Did what?"

"Oo'd."

"I shouldn't think so." Graham said. "They couldn't really get their things together with bellies like theirs."

There was much mirth at this.

"They couldn't any way," I said, with a sense of settling the matter, "because I was in between them."

"They might not have noticed," Norma squealed, and she and Graham went into fits.

I felt my face grow hot and red.

"Never mind, duck," Norma said, tousling my hair. I pulled my head away.

"Any way," she pursued, "I suppose it's too late now."

"Too late for what?" Graham asked.

"For you to have a brother or sister. Me mam says God doesn't allow it before you're twenty-one and after you're forty."

"That's not what I heard," Graham scoffed. "Mary Mahoney had a baby when she was fourteen."

"It must have been adopted then," Norma was very certain of her sources of information in these matters. "Like you." She put her fingers to her mouth to mock-suppress a snigger.

It was Graham's turn to go hot and red, though I didn't understand why. He stuffed his hands in his pockets and shrugged, turning aside so that we should not see his face. The trousers stretched tight across his broad bottom and thighs. He suddenly seemed to be nearly a youth and leaving me far behind in childhood.

"What did Uncle Wilf call these stones?" he asked, to change the subject.

Norma's answer didn't change it.

"The Bridestones," she smirked. "Let's get married."

"Ooh yes," I cried, "and I'll be your little lad."

This was a part I was used to taking in the play of older children, but

"No," said Norma firmly. "You can't be our little lad if we're not married yet. We've got to have the wedding first. You'll have to be the vicar."

I gave a grimace. This was not how I saw myself.

"Let Graham be the vicar and me and you get married."

"Don't be so daft. You're too little."

This made me feel even smaller than I was, and I wondered why vicars could be small, but husbands couldn't.

"Look, duck, it's easy," Norma cajoled, putting her arm round my shoulder so that I smelt the motherish smell of her armpit. "All you 've to do is say 'I pronounce thee man and wife' and put this ring on me finger."

"It's already on your finger."

"I know, but - " she twisted the ring and licked her knuckle to slip it off, "a wedding isn't proper without a ring."

I had some difficulty pronouncing "pronounce" and in my nervousness said "man and wipe", but Norma was radiantly happy. Really she was the celebrant and the mistress of ceremonies. She entered zestfully into all the roles and organised the procession while I played an imaginary organ and Norma and I sang "Here Comes the Bride". Norma gathered a confetti of leaves and petals which I then threw at the couple. Only the bride was truly happy, smiling like someone already in her dream world. Graham was visibly uncomfortable, worried perhaps in case the dream gave birth to something unlooked for. It did, for

"Kiss me now," the girl commanded, having appointed me as photographer.

Graham frowned.

"Do I have to?"

"Yes. A wedding isn't a wedding unless the groom kisses the bride."

He gave her a perfunctory peck and wiped his mouth afterwards, but she seemed even more radiant and proudly linked his arm for the procession to the Bridestones. She hummed the Wedding March and at the threshold stone she stood, and made Graham stand, in silence for a few moments as if absorbing something from the earth. Then they tiptoed carefully between the snoring elders, and I was left behind, having no further part to play. I felt excluded and forlorn, jealous too, and yearning for I knew not what. I wandered further on to the moorland, drawn by its dour loneliness that corresponded to my own. The harebells, the heather and the red rock spoke to me of something I was about to leave behind. It was only for a moment that I heard their voices, then the moment was gone, and I sank down sobbing my heart out.

It was Graham who came and comforted me, doing what Mamma so often had done for me, putting his ragged handkerchief to my tongue and wiping my cheeks with my own spit.

"Where's Norma?"

He shrugged.

"How should I know? She's daft, she is. She wanted me to oo 'er."

"Why didn't you?"

"You shouldn't 've told her about Maureen Foster. It put ideas into her head. I had to tell her what me mam said about cousins having funny babies."

This cheered me up no end. When we went back to the Bridestones, the elders were awake and packing up to go. Now it was Norma's turn to look lonely and withdrawn. She hardly spoke through all the journey back into the westering sun. It gave a glow to her bent head and I somehow felt sorry for her. It burnished the horse's back and made Prince's eyes look like marbles and put more fire into the Greatbatches' already incarnadined faces. It glistened on the barrage balloons and picked out the rock formations of Cloud End and Mow Cop in high relief. It turned the juice-misted fields into a sea in which trees sailed and slow-motion herds swam.

When the time came for the holidaymakers to leave the farm because of me, I found myself in the two minds that seemed to characterize the rest of my life. I was glad to be going home to Mamma and Dadda and Jimmy - it seemed years since I had seen them - but I also felt as though I was losing something good and it was losing me. I wanted to stay where I was and also to go on to the next thing. Then, when Mr Reynolds drew up in his Morris, twinkling and pipe-adjusting and infinitely tolerant, and when at last we were all packed in, I saw Norma still looking hopelessly abandoned. Instead of triumph that now I should be getting Graham all to myself again, I felt what she felt in losing him. But, as the car rolled us tipsily back into the Potteries, and Prince yelped with joy at coming home, I remembered that you - the only girl who really mattered after all - would be there to welcome me.

Maureen: After and *Before*

"Maureen's in the chapel. She's been there since Mass this morning and wouldn't come out even for her lunch. Perhaps you can persuade her. She seems to think we're the Gestapo."

The nun showed him to the chapel door. It was in a part of the building he had not entered before. Though he was familiar with many great churches in Catholic Europe, he hardly ever entered R.C. churches in Britain: like nonconformist chapels, they would be too new and strictly   for the sect.

However, despite being "adapted" for ecumenical use, the chapel still retained what was to him the essence of a Catholic church: space rendered as semi-darkness and permeated by ages of incense. But where were the clusters of candle-flames, the light-within-darkness, to suggest dimensions beyond the man-made walls? Gone, presumably, when the nuns gave up their house to its secular use. Not seeing Maureen in the gloom, he tiptoed up to the altar which had nothing on it but a routine flower-arrangement, probably artificial. The saints in the late Victorian windows gazed down forlornly at a banner which proclaimed that the millennium was Christ's 2000th birthday.

Jack turned back to the body of the church. His eyes having adjusted, he saw Maureen huddled before the Sacred Heart, a crudely painted statue pointing to a crimson heart whose generous size would have had modern surgeons reaching for their by-pass cutlery. Was she praying or worshipping? What a strange word - worship. Was she worshipping God for His gift of dementia or praying for the only possible release from it? Did she remember that she had become a Catholic on her marriage to Ray? Did she even know she was a Catholic, and if she didn't, was she? Had conversion meant anything more than permission to marry the man whose body she once worshipped? Religion hadn't figured much in her life before the wedding, but of course Jack knew nothing of her life in Australia.

Maureen: After and *Before*

As he slipped into the pew beside her he noticed that her fingers were telling the beads of a rosary and her mouth was forming soundless words. At first she did not react to his presence, but soon her breathing and the restlessness of her limbs began to express irritability.

"What the bloody 'ell are you doing in my house?"

"It's God's house," he whispered, feeling silly for saying so.

"Whose?"

"God's."

"You must think I'm daft. They're trying to take it away from me. But I've got the deeds. They're in that cupboard over there."

Her finger pointed at the disused aumbry to the side of the altar. As her hand was raised the rosary chain glinted in the gloom.

"If you say so."

"I do say so."

It was an interesting question - did God actually wish to possess all these "houses" of different religions and denominations that were said to be His? And if there were no God, then whose were they? The diocese's? The community's? Were they nationalised or privatised? The place was as much Maureen's as anybody's. Was it indeed anybody's now that it was non-denominational?

"Would you like to go back to your room now?"

"This is my room. I want to die here."

It seemed a reasonable desire. Always there seemed to be a sort of logic in what she said. Always he felt that to apply conventional reason was to exercise a futile tyranny. Maureen had reached a quasi-saintly stage in which the temporal world had ceased to matter. This was, if anywhere on earth was, the only possible kind of room for her to inhabit, where, like a medieval anchoress, walled up in relentless devotion, she would be sensed praying and squinting behind her screen, a solid gold guarantee to the passing congregations that what they tried to believe in really did exist. Thus, by asserting that her soul was God's, she made it truly her own. Jack should have left her, therefore, in possession, but pride tempted him: the nuns, he told himself, were relying on him to get her out of here.

"You aren't going to die for a long time. Meanwhile, wouldn't you like a cup of tea?"

"Yes, I would." It seemed all too easy, and it was. "You can go and fetch me one," she added. "I'd rather drink it here than be sitting round with all those bloody imbeciles."

"Oh - well - alright."

"So what're you waiting for? Go and get me that tea."

She settled further into her pew with awful solidity. Defeated, he went and confessed his failure to the nun who said grimly,

"Then we shall have to use brute force, I suppose."

"Can I take her a cup of tea first?"

"I'm sorry. The rules are, no eating or drinking in unauthorized places."

What about eating and drinking Jesus, he was tempted to ask. Instead, compounding his cowardice,

"I'd best get going," he said. "I don't want to be associated with the brute force."

"Oh, don't worry, it's not really that brutal. This sort of thing often happens. She'll forget about the chapel as soon as she's out of it."

Hurrying to get away, he saw that already two strong orderlies had been summoned, and he fancied, even as he dashed to his car, pursued by the thought that he was leaving her in the lurch, he could hear Maureen's cries of protest as she was wrenched from her haven. And it was no consolation to know that the lurch was the defining condition of old age, and that one day, perhaps soon, he would be left in it himself.

Maureen: After and Before

Maureen: After and Before

You came from a household where religion didn't figure: Cara merely shrugged when you said we were "going to Sunday School because there was nothing else to do." My parents were sardonic when I told them, Mamma because she had been brought up "church-not-chapel" and Dadda because he thought all religion "tummy-rot". However, they were happy for me to be occupied when they were "having five", as they called retiring to bed on Sunday afternoons. It seemed to me an odd habit but they, too, so they assured me, had nothing else to do. Some parents, of course, made their children go to Sunday School, so that they would be out of the way on Sunday afternoon.

Sunday School pupils were expected to have "Anniversary New" for the Whitsuntide ceremonies. That year Ida Lidgett made you a dark blue velvet frock whose skirt you could twirl in, and Mamma bought me a "tweed coat". I loved to see you in your frock and hated to see myself in my coat. How could I wear a winter's coat in May? Mamma said it had to do for every occasion, having cost her as much worry as money. Its hard hairy touch and dismal green-grey, so different from your rich blue velvet, really depressed me.

I was, therefore, not looking forward to the Anniversary Thanksgiving when we were to stand in the choir-gallery and bawl our gratitude for all God's gifts around us. But besides having new there were other preparations, such as getting one's Attendance Card marked up to date, with a blue ink star for a day, a silver for a month and gold for a complete year. You and I never got golds, because on fine Sundays we abandoned God for Nature, but occasionally we managed silver.

Our teachers read us Bible stories and made us promise to be good. While we were in their company we were very good, better than we were at our weekday school, even though the Sunday teaching was less than elementary and method non-existent. These spinsters-in-training made no effort to project their material. They did not need to: their faith commanded total submission. The interest was all in the way they looked as they read, tracing with a forefinger, their black Testaments. One sniffed and swallowed snot as she spoke in an adenoidal monotone; another wore pebble glasses and leaned far forward to peer at us as if unsure whether we were there or not. Our favourite was Miss Foote who kept curling her top lip back under her nostrils to produce a sort of snout, thus giving us something to imitate. She was gaunt and lugubriously fascinating, always dressed in a dark blue mackintosh which she never took off in our presence. She might have been, but almost certainly wasn't, naked underneath. Her pronouncements were as infallible as any Pope's, even when she wasn't speaking ex cathedra, the cathedra in this case being a high hard narrow chair, much like herself, the incarnation of woodenness.

She told us that the Anniversary was not meant just for dressing ourselves up: the chapel had to be dressed up too, because it was where God lived. I looked around and thought it was going to be a big job. Fancy God living here, between the canal and the sherd-ruck, in this squat brick building with its wooden steeple like exotic headgear on a dirty old man. Inside, gauntness and lugubriousness spread about Miss Foote like a web she had spun from the centre of her belief. Actual webs draped like dusty sails at the windows, which were of patterned blue and yellow glass. The columns supporting the gallery were of cream-painted iron but showed more rust than paint. The air smelt of escaping gas and trapped dust, and of damp plaster getting damper all the time. I liked it, especially when the winter sun tried to get through the glass to make patterns on the knobbly floorboards. Then you could actually see the air: a yellow-grey slant of compressed cloud. We pupils were a chaos of amoebic life at swim in this late Georgian geometry in which God lived and from which, Miss Foote said, He watched all our doings with a view to punishment, even when we were in the dark and particularly in the lavatory.

So we had to propitiate Him by bringing Him gifts which, we were told, He had given us in the first place. It was like the Harvest Festival at church, but this was May-time. You could bring fruit, flowers, cereals, processed cheese, or even tins of Spam which didn't seem to have passed through God's hands first. I chose flowers. But, having a father who was no gardener, I had to visit the nearest allotment and persuade a holder to part with his precious blooms. The allotments had a mock-rural setting - a curving green field on which sheep grazed, though not safely. The field was edged by high railings, being where animals spent their last night before execution at the abattoir. They munched their way over the windy pasture as if they were still on their home heaf, not knowing what lay ahead of them, not realising that there was no point in eating any more.

"Lamb of God," I murmured, thinking simultaneously of loin chops spitting fat under the grill, and a picture of Jesus that went under that name on the Sunday School wall.

I wandered up and down the rows of town flowers and vegetables, and passed from hut to hut in search of a gardener. The sheep stood solidly off-white and unaware of how accusatory they were, their short fat tails wagging between their meaty thighs.

The first man I approached for flowers said,

"Neow bloody fear," when I told him they were for a chapel.

The second turned his back and stepped inside his hut as soon as I uttered my first word. Then he closed the door and, lighting his pipe, watched me through the grimy hut-window till I left his patch. A third told me, with a jerk of his bulbous sweating head, to

"See Fred Moorby - he's over theer."

Fred Moorby was bending double at, and looking much like a growth from, a furrow of his soil. Instead of bending back up when I called,

"Ey mister, wou't sell us some flowers?" He simply spread his legs wide and spoke between them from his upside down face.

"What foer?"

"Our anniversary."

The man eased up, pushing his fist into the small of his back as if to release a spring. His face was as rough and crinkly as an old cauliflower.

"Yer anniversary?" So 'ow long 'ast tha been married? Tha'rt a bit young be married, tha knowst."

I was nonplussed. I guessed he was pulling my leg but I didn't know how to deal with such talk.

"I'm not married. It's for our Sunday School."

"Which one?"

"Baptist."

"In the name of th' fayther, th' son and th' owly ghoost Aymen."

The wry face laughed on its wryer neck. A gnarled finger pointed at a row of wall-flowers.

"Tha cust 'ave theyse fur sixpence or - " he swerved round and pointed at an almost identical row - "tha cust 'ave theyse fur - " he paused for maximum effect - "sixpence."

My gaze switched from one row to the other as if appraising

manifest differences. I settled on the first and handed over my sixpence. Having gathered them, the man then gathered the other row and bound the whole lot with a raffia twine. It was a nosegay for a giant and I had to hold it full in my arms so that the flowers blocked my vision and stifled my breath.

"Here," the man said as I turned, and he slipped the sixpence back into my pocket. "Those gillies 're nearly over. Thee'll ondly last a dee or teow - long enough for an anniversary though."

I stepped carefully away, unable to see the ground under my feet, my nose nestling in red, gold and brown petals and dewy sweetness all the way home.

My mother was impressed.

"He must have taken a fancy to you - or p'raps it was because they're for the chapel."

"He said they're nearly over."

"Oh well, that explains it." She was always grimly satisfied when ulterior motives were revealed. "People don't give something for nothing."

"Twasn't for nothing," I lied. "I paid sixpence for them."

"Well, it's your money."

I had hoped she might think it was her money and re-imburse me, but all she did was put the flowers in a bucket of water to keep them fresh till after dinner.

I ate quickly, eager to be off to the chapel with my wonderful gift for God and hoping nobody would notice that I was wearing a tweed coat in May. It was a business keeping the wet flower-stems away from it, and I was hot when I arrived. I proudly handed over my offering, and Miss Foote put it with the others on the dais. There it looked less impressive, since others had also brought wall-flowers. It was one of those moments that happen throughout life: you think yourself unique, original; then you find you are just one of many.

The procession was already forming. Miss Foote handed out the collecting boxes. The Boys' Brigade led us round the streets. We sang our hymns, rattled our boxes under people's noses and knocked on the Sunday-shut doors. I marched along, trying to give a summery swagger to my coat.

Recognised as an inseparable duo, you and I went collecting together. I don't suppose you'll mind my telling you now that I was wary of knocking at doors with you. You had a nasty habit of knocking just for the hell of it and running away just before the door opened, leaving me standing there gaping and speechless. Or alternatively, if, having got wise to your girlish ways, I ran away myself, you would stand and point at my cowardly retreat, informing the householder,

"It was him as knocked."

But on this occasion we were agents of God and had the right to knock without fear. Everybody knew we were about by the din the Brigade kicked up: crash, bang, wallop, thud. Dogs backed away and barked on springy haunches; cats streaked up to the coping stones of walls and licked themselves back to dignity, old men re-arranged the cotton wool in their ear-holes, and solitary ladies twitched their curtain nets and stood behind them, untouchable and all-seeing as harem-wives. You would not have thought we were believers in the Day of Rest and our chapel affiliated to the Lord's Day Observance Society. At intervals we stopped collecting and assembled for our hearty hymn, rattling our tins with the tambourines to show each other and God how well we were doing. Money was music to our ears.

You and I made a smart move and got ahead of the procession. We turned into Palmerston Street where my 'Eight o' Clock Mother' lived. You remember Aggie Dunkley? I called her my eight o'clock mother because every weekday morning Mamma presented me to her just before going to work. Aggie was a round soft quiet woman who would open the door still in her nightie and nursing her latest baby. She had weeping eyes from duct-trouble, and weeping legs from too much baby-bearing, the present one being her fifth. Your mother and mine agreed that Mr Dunkley was to blame because he wouldn't "leave Aggie alone." This was puzzling, since Mamma also complained that my father "leaves me on my own too much". No wonder, with such a fine balance to be struck, a good husband was, as women often said, "hard to come by". I rarely saw Mr Dunkley as he had always gone to work before I arrived. But I did see, through the open parlour door, his bagpipes perched like a stranded octopus on the settee. They were his pride and joy and he played them with a band of Scots exiles wearing kilt and sporran, though he was, my mother ambiguously vowed, "no more Scotch than an oatcake."

I would stay with the Dunkleys till nine o'clock when four of her six sons - Cyril, Jamie, Gordon and Bob - escorted me to our weekday school. I shared their breakfast and their comics. The lads would lure me into the back yard and then lift stones to show me worms, centipedes and earwigs. I wanted to see them even though, or because, they made my flesh creep and even though Gordon would pick one up and throw it at me. I then ran back indoors "squealing", as he said with satisfaction, "like a tart".

All the boys treated tarts, including their mother, with contempt.

Maureen: After and Before

Her life was one long chore cooking, cleaning, washing and ironing for what my mother called "six selfish pigs", though some of them were mere piglets. If only one of them had been a girl, my mother contended, Aggie's life would have turned out differently. Or, if only she didn't have to put up with Mr Dunkley who, apparently, was "never satisfied". On the few occasions on which I did see him this permanent dissatisfaction expressed itself in his curt sandy moustache, his drill sergeant manner and, above all, in the way he practised on his pipes.

    Standing now in front of the Dunkleys' house, way ahead of the Anniversary procession, I experienced conflict. You were urging me to knock at the door, saying reasonably,

"They're friends of yours, aren't they?"

But this was the trouble. It was easier to beg money from strangers. I felt all of a lather in my winter coat. I tapped the knocker timidly.

"They're out." Thank God, I added under my breath.

"I don't think so. People seem to be out on Sunday afternoon - but they're usually in bed."

"P'raps they're having five."

"That's what they call it." You smiled to yourself as you always smiled when you knew something I didn't.

I tried to move us on to the next door, but,

"Look through there," you commanded, pointing to the letter-slit under the knocker. "I'll lift you up."

You lifted me off my feet without waiting for my assent. I raised the knocker and peered through. There was no sign of life, just the comfortable Sunday-gravy smell that issued from most houses after dinner.

"They can't all be having five" you said. "Lads don't have five."

"They'll be playing football in the park. There's a key hanging down inside here." I wanted to show off my privileged knowledge and immediately wished I hadn't.

"Then fetch it out for goodness' sake and we'll open the door."

I was dubious.

"Put me down."

"They won't mind you." You showed no sign of putting me down.

So I drew out the key inch by inch. You took it avidly and turned the lock. The door opened, like one in a fairy story, on to a silent house. Automatically, being in my home from home, as I passed the coat-hooks in the little passage, I slipped off my coat and hung it up. It was a relief to be rid of it. We tiptoed towards the living room, passing the open parlour door and the bagpipes sitting on the settee. We froze as we became aware of a whispering voice coming from upstairs.

"Dunna do it again, duck, no dunna. No, Ken, please dunna. I conna stand no more. Doctor says I munna. Dunna, duck."

I knew that voice, ineffectual as it was insistent.

"It's Mrs Dunkley," I hissed. Then

"You'll do as you're bloody well told, woman," came Mr Dunkley's sergeant major tone.

"No, duck, please, Ken, no."

"I'm going to give it you right this minute."

"He's murdering her," you said. "We'd best be off."

And you made for the door, leaving me in an agony of indecision. How could I go and leave my eight o'clock mother to be murdered? How could I stay and not be murdered too? As so often I dithered and did nothing, but stood helpless halfway up - or halfway down - the stairs. The door closed with a bang behind you. I was on my own. At which the woman's voice suddenly changed its tone, saying,

"What was that? Did you 'ear that door go? If those lads 've - "

Then a figure came flying on to the landing in a ghostly nightgown, shrieking,

"What in 'eaven's name? Who's there? You!"

It was Aggie herself - yet not herself, for she spoke to me as she had never spoken before.

"Who let you in, you little tripe-'ound? What the devil d'you mean barging in 'ere without so much as a by-your-leave?"

Aggie Dunkley reared over me. The soft, mild white-smocked angel had become a strident gnashing demon, her hair wild around her fat puffy shoulders and her huge soft breasts flapping in her nightie-front. There was an inexplicable but vaguely familiar smell about her.

"I only came for the Anniversary," I stammered.

She was stopped in her tracks.

"Anniversary?" she queried, baffled.

At that moment the procession rounded the corner of Palmerston Street - crash, wallop, boom. Another figure appeared on the landing - Kenneth Dunkley, his shirt just decent above his hairy, wiry legs.

"What the bloody 'ell? he yelled. And the band stopped playing. There was a brief silence to which we all listened far more intently than to any sound, and then a hymn started up for the Palmerston Street residents. Mr Dunkley listened, as if appraisingly, for a few moments, then, dashing past his wife and me, he made for the parlour and came out with his pipes. He threw open the front door and, after preliminary puffs and squeezes and several false starts, he began to play, parading up and down the passage and drowning out the Jubilee hymn. The choir of teachers and pupils and the instrumentalists of the Boys' Brigade, subjugated into silence, stood there open-mouthed. Then, suddenly abandoned, the pipes groaned and collapsed on the settee as if breathing their last, and the player turned his sinewy neck round at me.

"Get!" He pointed at the open door.

I got. It was only when we were processing out of Palmerston Street and into Pelham Road that you asked me what I'd done with my new coat. It was still on Dunkleys' hook!

You gripped your bottom lip with your front teeth and, with staring eyes, said,

"Well, you can't ever go back there."

I thought it was all your fault and refused to go on collecting with you. As a result I only collected two and ninepence and offered it to God and Miss Foote with tears starting from my eyes.

"Never mind," she said, and, after making a snout with her top lip, added, "Every little helps."

"Where's your coat?" were my mother's first worried words when I got in. "You haven't gone and left it at the Baptist for somebody to run off with?"

I burst into tears. My brother Jimmy looked at me compassionately:

"I'll run down there and fetch it," he offered.

"No," I panicked. "Miss Foote's got it."

"Why?"

I cast about for inspiration.

"Because I was too hot. She's keeping it for the Thanksgiving Service tonight."

My mother still looked vexed. I couldn't explain - I thought it would vex her even more to know what had happened at the Dunkleys'.

I had been called a tripehound and I had been cursed and expelled by an angel. Mercifully, my family wasn't interested in evangelical entertainments and so didn't see me giving unthankful thanks, amid the new-clothed choir, in my old grey jersey. I deliberately kept my distance from you, so smart in your blue velvet which Ida Lidgett had trimmed for you with white lace. I assumed that everybody was focussing on my lack of "new" and thinking my parents too mean or worse, too poor, to care. In fact, as Mamma predicted, people were only interested in their own appearance - a lesson one never seems to learn.

I tried to concentrate, as Miss Foote had said we should, on the sermon of the Preacher from Oswestry, though I was more interested in his Welsh accent, his nutmeg-like head, and the way he kept unhooking his pince-nez with pernickety thumb and middle finger. Besides, I had doubts about his qualifications: he couldn't really be a reverend because he wore a Norfolk jacket and an ordinary collar and plaid tie. Some of his words, however, got through to me. He said the service was the offering of first fruits, though there was hardly any fruit to be seen, and he raised a chapel-hollow titter when he spoke of us children as "first fruits", most of us being second or third crop.

He turned in a crescendo of excitement to the subject of human sacrifice offered, as he swingeingly put it, "By benighted barbarous Pagan tribes of the pre-Pentateuch era."

Even Father Abraham (he pronounced the name impressively with a short flat initial "A" and a long "harm" at the end) was willing to sacrifice his own son Isaac (pronounced "Eezark"), but God's own angel held his arm. And from then on animals were sacrificed instead. Which didn't strike us kids as an advance in civilisation. I thought of the sheep on the allotment field. We had already heard the Isaac story from Miss Foote and raised this and other doubts. Why hadn't Isaac's mother stepped in to save her boy? Why did God leave intervening till the last minute? Wouldn't the boy have died of fright? The whole story seemed a tangle of contradictions, yet we wanted to hear it over and over again, because the idea of being sacrificed by one's father was so terrible and compelling.

The Reverend Morgan moved to his peroration: it concerned the tongues of flame that descended on the apostles when Jesus left them. Again Miss Foote had already dealt with this and with our consequent queries: who was the Holy Ghost the ghost of, and were the tongues still around, ready to descend on anybody, even us?

"Only if you're perfect," Miss Foote had replied, adding with sepulchral contralto emphasis, "Be ye therefore perfect even as your Father in Heaven is perfect."

Yet, on another occasion, she had said, "Nobody's perfect". I sighed

ing the gauze in place, wrapped the leg in a fresh new bandage, and rolled the stocking back into place.

"There, it'll be as right as rain now, though I don't know why rain is right when we have so much of it." She unwrapped a barley sugar sweet and popped in into Maureen's ready mouth.

Maureen then put her hand to the nun's free arm and tugged at the grey rolled-up cardigan sleeve. The nun bent, as indicated by Maureen's other hand, to kiss the offered cheek. Maureen's smile was like the smile of the blessed. I wish I could do that, he thought. I wish I could kiss her without disgust or fear. Fear of women was it, or fear of age and death? The nun, no doubt, had kissed any number of disgusting bodies without qualm, because the bodies were only outer shells of infinitely beautiful souls. There it was again, that word. The soul, wrapped within the body wrapped within its bonds. Why did Lazarus come back from the dead? He recalled the unwinding of a mummy in an old horror film. Was it possible that Maureen's legs would be unbandaged to dance again in another world?

"Friday night," you used to say, "is Amami night," the night when your cousin Lorna washed her hair ready for love on Saturday. She washed yours too, though you weren't quite ready for love at that stage. It was also the night when I had my weekly bath, in front of the kitchen fire and in front of Mrs Edwards. Mrs Edwards visited us on Friday evenings, and Mamma and I went to see her on those Saturdays when my father was working the late shift. Mrs Edwards had a little shop and was said to be "on the change". I waited for this change to take place before my eyes. I never minded about her watching me being bathed, but I couldn't understand why she wanted to, since it always made her cry. Eventually I got used to women wanting to do things that made them cry. Every time my mother lifted me out and sat me on her knee to dry me, Mrs Edwards cried. She cried because she was reminded of her own son when he was a lad. Maurice was now on active service with a bomb disposal unit.

Sometimes she would beg,

"Let me dry him."

It did not seem strange to me to be handed from one woman to the other, to have my shuddering body rubbed back to warmth. Mrs Edwards was very particular about drying between the toes as

"They get foot-and-mouth else," she laughed through her tears.

When I complained that my bottom itched,

"P'raps he's got worms," she suggested.

She put me on my belly over her knee and the two women examined me. When I was set upright again they looked at each other and laughed.

"It's not funny," I said, offended that other people could see a part of me - and particularly that part - I couldn't see myself.

Mrs Edwards's laughter always turned to tears. She cried a lot, especially on Saturday evening, when Mamma and I fetched brown ale from the Off-License. Mrs Edwards paid for it from the shop-till, whose drawer flirted open of its own accord, even after Mrs Edwards had firmly shut it and wagged a warning finger at it.

In a repetitive conversation over the beer Mrs Edwards spoke of her late husband, which also made her cry. My ears pricked up when she said she felt like walking under a bus. When I asked Mamma why Mrs Edwards wanted to walk under a bus, she replied sharply,

"It's only talk. People who say they'll do that never do."

It was news to me that anybody said it let alone did it, and later I told my pals I felt like walking under a bus just to make sure I never did it.

I was more interested in Mrs Edwards's home, however, than I was in Mrs Edwards, because, although it was in the middle of a terraced row and otherwise identical with those around it, the front room was a miniature store selling tea, sugar, sweets, aspirins, tinned stuff and a few feeble vegetables. Everything, in fact, looked feeble, as did Mrs Edwards herself, but this was the kind of shop I dreamed of having, with a small netted window between it and the living-room, so that customers could be seen entering and, if necessary, watched. There was also, on a curly iron bracket, a bell whose twang signalled entry and exit. Under the primitive cash register there was an even more primitive dealwood drawer, with a sloping bottom and an outlandish odour. Here were kept the IOU's which, before the war, Mrs Edwards had accepted more often than money and were yet another source of tears for her.

It was a privilege to pass behind the oil-clothed counter and to handle the set of beautiful worn brass weights that were arranged on it. Extra magic was added by twilight, the shop windows being without black-out. The odour that met me in the gloom was that of my own imagination, richer than the melange of what was actually there. I should have loved to dwell forever in those heady shadows, tracing the shapes of the weights and weaving my thoughts round the barely visible merchandise. First, though, I had to sit for a while with the two women in the hot living-room, listening to their talk and glancing up now and then at the small window that looked into the invisible world.

There was some compensation in the glass of American Ice Cream Soda that Mrs Edwards gave me. There was also her bed, kept downstairs because of air raids. It had a quilt whose over-stuffed corners I picked at to blow feathers at the cats. Tommy and Maudie were sister and brother, though they seemed not to know it, or at least not the taboo on incest, and were named after two radio stars, one a comedian, the other a comedienne, though they didn't know that either. They belied their names, being mostly idle and unsociable, opening one eye apiece when we entered and putting their paws up round their faces to shut out the unwanted intrusion. But sometimes Mrs Edwards gave them a sup of ale to make them "run up a straight wall".

That made her laugh till, again, she cried. I laughed too, but felt cheated. They didn't really run up the walls, not to the ceiling any way, but at least the beer transformed them into kittens again, and they raced round in circles after their own or each other's tails, and clawed their way up the curtains which were, like Mrs Edwards's nerves, in shreds. They behaved rather like people when drunk, loosely and foolishly, to the wary mirth of the sober.

"Ooh the Name!" Mrs Edwards would cry, and

"Whatever next?" my mother would ask of the ceiling as if the Name might be written there. Mrs Edwards always said "the Name" when she meant God, which made me wonder what His name actually was.

Unfortunately the ale did not have as violent an effect on the women as it did on the cats. It made them talk endlessly about the various kinds of anguish that women had to suffer because of men. This made me, little man in the making, feel very guilty, especially when Mrs Edwards vouchsafed in a whisper that she was "very small-made" whereas her husband had been "very big-made". I didn't know what this meant but it seemed to have been another mistake on God's part. It was when the talk got round to Maurice and his bomb-disposing that Mrs Edwards declared that she would like to walk under a bus.

Rather than listen I preferred to explore the other two ground floor rooms, Mrs Edwards didn't mind as long as I didn't break anything. The cats would also disappear, sidling round the skirting board and through the shredded chenille curtain to the shop where they would insinuate themselves between the Rinso and the Liver Salts.

In the shop I edged drawers open and sniffed inside cupboards and, if I had remembered to bring my precious torch, see what was under the counter. So much in those days was said to be "under the counter" that I was disappointed to find only further supplies of the things that stood on the shelves behind it. Mrs Edwards was, also disappointingly, no Black Marketeer. In fact, she was terrified of doing the wrong thing and having the Ministry of Food breathing down her neck. The war and being "on the change" had made her, in her own words, "nothing but a bag of nerves".

I specially liked to rummage in the box containing 'small items'

Maureen: After and Before

- streamers for Christmas, that concertina'd from a flat base into crinkled swags of colour; and birthday cards in shiny number-shapes, showing children who actually lived the life one wanted to live, with model yachts on ponds, and gardens with sun-dials, bird-tables and super-real roses.

After feeling round the nooks and crannies of the shop, I settled down with the cats to stare from the window on the street. The windows were criss-crossed with tape, so the view even in summer was restricted. There wasn't much to see any way, only the grimy terrace opposite and the pot-bank chimneys behind it, and perhaps a few kids at late play, making me wonder which I preferred: being indoors with the wise and silent cats or out there with my own kind, boisterous and silly. Sometimes the ARP wardens practised their emergency drill and unrolled their hoses, running with them on wheels from the hydrant, a vast open air bath filled not just with water but also fascinating scum, dust, litter and unmentionable submerged objects. The ARP wardens, being oldish men and youngish women, took ages to get their stirrups pumping and, as my father snorted,

"Whole bloody town'd be ashes before they even turned their taps on."

The best evenings of all were when I caught a glimpse of you and your cousin Lorna with her first boyfriend in the twilight. She was plump and blonde with large blue eyes. He was callow and pimply, with brilliantined hair and a tendency to blush for no apparent reason. You watched their behaviour and I, an avid voyeur from my dark vantage point, watched yours. I could not understand it then and perhaps only half-understand it now. I suppose you were learning the technique that girls had to learn in those days: how to seduce the male and at the same time keep him at bay. Your mother had taught you the theory, and Lorna, now aged fifteen, was showing you the practice. But even then I could see that you - at not more than eleven - wanted to practise it too. You did everything in your power to capture the boy's attention. When he sat on the yard-wall you plonked yourself on his knee, and stayed there till Lorna pushed you off. You tweaked his tie out of his pullover, and from his pocket you deftly tweaked his handkerchief, running in triumph down the street, the handkerchief streaming white and he puffing red behind you, while Lorna stood in dudgeon, hands on hips. The hands stayed on the hips when he returned to her, and she leaned forward at him, mouthing what to me were soundless scoldings as in a silent film. In fact it was as good as being at the pictures, for suddenly the callow youth stopped her mouth with a kiss. You stood halfway down the street, and I knelt in the shop's shadows, both of us watching them, transfixed. For Lorna's fury had turned to molten desire. She raised her face to his, and her Amami'd hair fell softly back. She raised one leg and let the back of her shoe fall away from her heel as if she were Alice Faye and the callow youth Don Ameche. I watched you as you watched them, and we were both witnesses of that pure incandescent Ultimate Kiss. It was like being in church, full of reverence, they the celebrants, you and I the awed communicants. I felt a thrill that not even wanking with Graham could give me. I was a part of that ecstasy, but which part was the question.

In a trance I wended my way out of the shop and into Mrs Edwards' back kitchen. It was warm and steamy. There was usually something simmering on the gas-stove: lobby or peas, beetroot, or barley water. This produced interesting odours as well as effects of gas and vapour. When the light was switched on, dimmed by red gauze in case German airmen could see Mrs Edwards cooking, I watched rivulets of seeming-sweat run down the butter-coloured top half of the wall into the bottle-green lower half.

Whenever I see condensation on dingy walls in dim light, I am taken back to one terrible evening and one terrible morning, not in immediate sequence of time but linked indissolubly one with the other. That evening - it seems like the last I was ever at Mrs Edwards's though I know it wasn't - I was performing my usual slow circuit of that back kitchen and savouring its contents. First there was the new-fangled enamel washer with its black-knobbed handle for mashing the clothes, then the old-fangled corner boiler built of brick with a lead bowl, like a primitive font, covered by a circular deal-wood top. I passed my fingers along the oil-clothed shelving and arrived at the low, shallow stone sink that smelt very drainish. I sniffed at the tin of soft soap kept under the sink to counter-act cat's turd, Mrs Edwards being not too particular about where they "did their business". I came at last to the gas-stove where tiny popping blue flames kept a saucepan of lentils simmering. I could not resist turning the tap ever so slightly to ensure that all the gas-holes stayed lit, as I did not want us to be gassed or blown up. The flames went from blue to yellow as drops of lentil-water hissed down the side of the pan, then flickered back to blue again.

What happened to me next was later referred to as all my own fault, but it wasn't really. I said it was the cats' fault, but you couldn't blame them either. One of them tripped me up and I snatched at a tea-towel that was hanging over the plate-rack to dry. The towel caught on the handle of the simmering pot, a yowling animal leapt out of the way, there was a moment's silence, then a soft crash and a piercing cry from me as the lentil slop sprayed and scoured its way over my left leg, searing and searching through my thin socks down to my foot. The air was all steam, lentils and scalded flesh.

If up to that moment Mrs Edwards had been a bag of nerves, the bag now burst. The two women rushed in, the dimmed light went on, I was picked up and carried screaming to the bed in the living-room. They managed to prise open my bunched body and, stretching me out, saw what had happened and did something the doctor said later should not have been done. They snatched off my socks. As the lentil-sticky, lentil-smelling wool peeled away, so did my skin, in long infinitely tender shreds that might have been Mrs Edwards's nerves, so stricken and so heart-broken was she on my behalf. We all three gazed in awe at the soft pink skin-skeins and the under-skin which looked like layered rose petals, but petals in pain.

"Oh the Name!" Mrs Edwards cried. "The poor little beggar! I shall never live through this. Oh the little soul!"

Her weeping made me weep all the more for my agonised flesh, yet somehow I saw it as belonging to someone else, just as I do now. The pain was atrocious, but it was partly happening outside of me. My mother fetched my father from the pub. He took me in his arms and dashed up the street with me to the doctor, who lived in a huge house and in some style but among his panel patients´ hovels. Dr Dain did all that was necessary, keeping his medicines, ointments and tinctures, like himself, on the spot. The skin was bathed in a borax solution and wrapped in lint and reams of bandage. Even the fluff of the lint was a torment. I cried and cried but enjoyed playing the central role in the drama. I also liked the clean whiteness and sterility of my strange new garment. My father carried me home and then up and down our long front passage-way, up and down, down and up, any number of times, till my sobbing softened to snuffles. But I started up again whenever he made to lay me in a chair. It seemed a long time since he had held me in his arms and just now that was where I most wanted to be.

For a while I was a fully conscious baby, pampered and never ignored. When large shiny blisters wobbled on my foot they were dusted with boracic powder, and Mrs Edwards came soothing with wads of cotton wool and yet more powder. Eventually the blisters silently exploded into shallow pink pools to be mopped up by the clouds of cotton wool and touched lightly with antiseptic cream also supplied by Mrs Edwards. The treatment almost made the agony worthwhile. The disinfected aura I dwelt in appealed to me , as did having my thin legs and little feet constantly attended to, not least by you, dear Maureen. You carried me about and indulged my whims as if I were a budding

Chinese emperor.

Everything turned out as the doctor said it would: the rawness became a soreness, an itchiness and then a mere tenderness, and eventually all that remained were silvery star-shapes on my skin, there to this day.

I was amazed and even disappointed to find myself back to normal. Not quite as I had been, however - I was more careful, more fearful, more anxious, more, it has to be said, like Mrs Edwards. From then on I became, as my mother put it, "highly strung", as if I were a musical instrument. But if it made me highly strung, my accident turned Mrs Edwards into a nervous wreck. My mother said she was "never the same woman", and that was why I felt responsible for what happened next.

You would certainly remember what happened next if you could remember anything, since it was the talk of the neighbourhood for a long time. I mean "next" in this narrative, of course, not in life. It was, maybe, many months later. You and I were playing hopscotch in the backyard when we heard a commotion in the street. We climbed the wall to see what it was, and there was a Police van parked outside Mrs Edwards's shop. Our first thought was that the Ministry of Food had caught up with her, and she was to be arrested and taken away to an unknown destination from which she would not return. You said this was what happened to Black Marketeers who kept things under the counter.

Small groups of spectators were assembling and there was a buzz of speculation, no more reliable than yours. The police shouted "No smoking!" and put on gas-masks as if an air-raid were in the offing. Some people rushed to fetch their own masks and missed the denouement.

A gloved policeman broke the glass of the shop-door and opened it from the inside. Two cats shot out as if fleeing from something unspeakable. The crowd drew back strained forward and backed again like the chorus in a musical. Could the house have been hit by a bomb in the night? But it was intact, and any way shouldn't we have heard it? The policeman came out at last carrying something that looked, although covered, like a body.

Mrs Edwards, instead of walking under a bus, had put her head in the gas-oven. She had fastened the cats in the shop and sealed herself in the dingy steamy back kitchen with the sweating walls.

"She was determined to do it," Mamma said, "one way or another."

I was baffled by this blatant contradiction of her previous views, but when she went on to add,

"Our Jacky's accident was the last straw,"

I was horrified and gazed at my blotched leg, which, though it looked as frail and pale and combustible as that last straw itself, assumed an awesome power in my eyes: the power to drive a fellow human being to her death. And why, I kept asking myself, had she chosen the gas-oven? Was it a kind of self-punishment because of what it had done to me?

In 1945 the Bomb Disposal Unit returned Maurice Edwards to his home more or less intact. He was minus one hand. His home, of course was not intact at all. The bereft little house now reverted to a purely domestic life, if life it could be called, though its front wall retained its tin advertisements till they became rust-blotched and unidentifiable. For a while Maurice set up a one-man window-cleaning business with his so-called gratuity. We kids would watch him going up and down ladders with the bucket handle hung on his hook, which was like an upside-down question mark where his hand should have been. The "good" hand mopped the windows with a bunch of chamois shreds. Outwardly Maurice was silent and stoical, but occasionally, when he was cleaning our windows, I would catch sight of his face on the other side of the glass. Behind the wash-leather flurries his features were tortured and his mouth worked with words I could not hear. Was it me he was cursing or was it, as now seems more likely, that inscrutable being whom his mother always invoked in her times of trial - namely, the Name?

One day he was at your back windows when your mother strode out of your house and shouted up the ladder at him.

'What the hell d' you think you're playing at, you bloody hound?'

Maurice nearly fell from his perch and only just managed to hook himself on to a rung. With painful deliberation he climbed down the ladder and gathered together the tools of his trade. He kept his face, working with its terrible silent words, averted from the woman and never showed it at her windows again.

What he had been playing at, so your mother told mine with a strange mixture of indignation and hilarity, was "pocket billiards, the cheeky bugger!" while he watched you changing your clothes in your bedroom. But how could he do that with both hands occupied in cleaning windows and one of them a hook? And why you were changing your clothes at that unlikely hour with the curtains wide open only you could tell. And now you never will.

Everything to do with you and your mother made me dissatisfied with being merely male. I wanted to be like you. I think I got as much pleasure out of clattering about in high heels as you did. But you were being hurried into womanhood. Whilst I, eternal child, was privy to the process, like a dwarf attendant on an odalisque.

You were preparing to be a sort of femme fatale, with all your mother's arts behind you. You were to fulfil her dream of "show business". To this end she sent you to Miss Libby's Tap Dance Studio. Nobody I asked knew or would say Miss Libby's other name, or whether Libby was her first. The secret seemed important and was kept even by her mother, who played the piano and took the money for the lessons and was herself known as Nona. She, too, referred to her daughter as Miss Libby. The name was set in a box above the front door. From the door, stairs went straight up to a first floor room which echoed with heavy hands on the piano and even heavier feet going bump slither thud on the bare floorboards. The dancers were all girls but, because I was "only little" (which admitted me over a number of forbidden thresholds) you took me along as a spectator. The long upper room, two bedrooms made into one, was lined with photographs of Miss Libby being hugged by celebrities such as Ronald Gourlay and Kitty McShane.

Miss Libby used a long wand and was a sharp disciplinarian. She had an Eton crop, and wore pointed glasses with glittering chains looping under her ears, and also black tights ending in pointed pumps. She carried a man's handkerchief to wipe her mouth from time to time. Somebody said she had consumption and sometimes spat on the floor and made girls do the splits over the bloodied gob. This I very much wanted to see. It never happened when I was there, but I did hear Miss Libby cough and noticed the frightened look her mother gave her. Nobody was allowed to help or sympathise, since help and sympathy were regarded as "unprofessional". You girls were training to become professionals or "semi-professionals" and so didn't get any sympathy either. Many a girl was reduced to tears and this seemed to make her into an instant "professional", for her dancing skills would improve dramatically from that moment on. At Miss Libby's, art was all that mattered.

She kept the local theatre supplied with a troupe called the Babes. They became so well known they appeared on the national pantomime circuit. Your mother, whose will was as ruthless as Miss Libby's, was determined that you should become a Babe. At first I could not understand this. I thought that babyhood was something even I had left behind. But soon I was as avid for you to become a Babe as your mother was. Something inside me craved for a fulfilment that could only be achieved through someone else, in fact through a girl. That girl was you.

At last, after a year or two of bump slither thud, correction by the witch-wand and many tears, you made it to the Big Time and appeared as one of the Babes in Cinderella. In the version of the story I knew there were no babies and I was eager to see where they fitted in. But my keenest interest was in Principal Boys. I much preferred the lean brunette Dandini to the blonde gross-hipped Prince. Both whacked their thighs with gusto, and both sets of legs started on heels higher even than your mother's, and then went, as Rita's Victor put it, "straight up to their arses". To my disgust the Ugly Sisters were men, fools of men at that, as if ugliness, foolishness and maleness were interchangeable. I felt affronted in my gender and confirmed in a growing conviction that pretty girls were what the world most wanted. You Babes were a wow, totally irrelevant to the plot but in precise drill, in the coordination of voice, leg and foot, and absence of all individual identity, a credit to your trainer. And when she came on stage, handkerchief to mouth, to acknowledge the applause, she beamed for once benignly. The wicked Witch had become the Fairy Godmother. I witnessed and was duly converted by the Triumph of Art. There seemed no way, however, that I could partake in that triumph. It was marked Females Only.

Then a new suppliant appeared at the shrine of dance: a boy! But this was no ordinary boy. In fact he was Mein Tan, Maylee's elder brother. We called him Minton. His coming brought another clash of loyalties. I began to worship Minton. But he took no notice of me. He was intent only on the dance, and when not dancing was so elusive as to impinge in no way whatsoever on anybody or anything. When he was dancing, however, one couldn't take one's eyes off him. There seemed to be no contortion that his body could not go into with ease. Added to which he had a perfect sense of rhythm and an unerring knowledge of how to please Miss Libby. She came to dote on him, much to the murmuring of the Babes. Minton became a star and you Babes had to play second fiddles. It was a thrilling sight when, dressed in his Rudolf Valentino outfit - matador hat, sequinned bolero, white shirt and long black trousers, tight as trousers were never known to be in those days - he led the troupe in Latin American formations. Rio Rita went wild over him.

"He's a real beaut!" she declared. "Did you see his little belly button going wiggle wiggle wiggle?"

I longed to wiggle my belly button and be called "a beaut". I wanted to be Minton, just as I had once wanted to be his sister! Yet what was allowed to and admired in him was forbidden to me. It was not just that my mother could not afford for me to have lessons from Miss Libby: it was that "Boys don't do that sort of thing."

"Minton Lu does," I pouted.

"Well, he's Chinese, isn't he?"

"Only half. What different does that make?"

"It's their nature."

"It's mine as well."

"Be told," my father put in, his tone and teeth-grinding face warning me not to persist.

But when next Christmas came and I went to the Panto again, there was Minton, heading the chorus line, a star. This time it was Aladdin which, given the liberties traditionally taken by Pantomime, was thought the ideal setting for a Chinese boy to lead you very British Babes in suave South American routines to wild applause. Riveted by his narrow brown-yellow belly writhing under his tied shirt, I experienced agonies of envy and love-longing. I was thoroughly confused about the roles I should have liked to play. No such agony or confusion affected Minton. He was all and only what he ever wanted to be, and had attained, at the age of thirteen, the nirvana of pure art. When Miss Libby came on the stage to embrace him, the Babes saw, for the first time in their dancing lives, tears streaming down her cheeks.

Not long after this, Miss Libby's studio closed: she had collapsed from a lung haemorrhage and was incarcerated in a sanatorium.

Early in the War my parents had acquired their first wireless set – second hand. It worked at the whim of a mysterious oblong glass vessel in its back parts, called an accumulator, which never gained, but always seemed to be losing, whatever it was supposed to accumulate. The leads of the vessel were wasted by a blue corrosion said to be caused by the acid lurking frighteningly behind the glass, like something eating at the Opera Phantom's face. There was a smell of dust and dirt trapped in fretted layers of metal, and sinister lightless bulbs called valves. But magical things came from the friendly walnut face of the set, including Victor Sylvester's do-it-yourself dance lessons. The directions were impossible to follow because, by the time my mind had registered the move and told my feet what it was, Victor Sylvester had already gone on to the next one. And there was absolutely no way of distinguishing quicksteps from foxtrots, or rumbas from sambas. However, I found the rhythms irresistible. My body wanted to move to music, even though it was a boy's and not Chinese. My family had become wireless-mad, so there was never a time when I could listen on my own. However, I found a space in the room where I thought I should be out of the way. There I pretended to myself that I was following Victor Sylvester's instructions to the letter. I was lost in dance. I sometimes tied my coat by its arms round my waist in imitation of a flaring skirt.

So absorbed and obsessed by my art did I become that I did not notice my father's mounting fury. One evening, unable to bear any longer what he called "this cissy stuff", in the midst of a luscious rumba he leapt up from behind his newspaper, switched off the wireless so violently that the knob came away in his hand, snatched my arm and dragged me to my knees. For the first time in my life I had the strap. I had once watched when Jimmy had it and it filled me with terror. It was one of those occasions when our father "looked what he was", eyes ablaze and mouth a-snarl. I rolled into myself like a hedgehog. It was not all that painful but it left me shuddering with incomprehension and scalded with tears. I looked for help to my mother, but she only watched and bit her lip, alienated from us both. The man stood back at last, in an anguish of pity and guilt. Then he turned on my mother.

"It's you!" he shouted. "It's you who've made him like this!"

I thought he was going to use the belt on her too. But he sank back into his chair and hid behind the newspaper, shaking and smacking it from time to time to show that he would not soften. In the past when he was cross with me, I had been able to woo him back with peeps and nudges, or just by bestriding his leg for a Ride a Cock Horse. But there was to be no more of that. I felt the lump in my throat harden to resentment. I did not know what this "this" was that he said I had been made like, or why it was so terrible.

How could I know that behind the irritability and the newspaper Dadda was suffering from an inevitable defeat? How could I sense his loneliness and impotence in a household that seemed to me to be his to command? How register the moment when I passed from the male sphere to the female?

Once, when Mamma was telling your mother about my dancing, Carrie nodded at me with a hard appraising look and said,

"You can see he's his mother's boy, can't you?"

It was not meant as a compliment but I was happy to take it as one.

"That's what the nurse at the Limes said he would be the day he was born. But -" Mamma sighed wistfully, " - he still loves his dadda, don't you?"

"I love him, but I don't like him." I guessed rightly that this would sound very impressive and didn't let on that I had heard it said in a radio play.

"Well, he's very cute, I must say!" Your mother looked me up and down, as if seeing a strange future for me. What she could not see was the change that a few years had wrought. As an infant I had loved my father unequivocally. But now I was afraid of him, my love for him had gone underground like a limestone river, ant it would only emerge in unexpected ways.

Dadda was partly right: my mother was making me "like this". But she was not alone. Everything my father did from now on pushed me further towards "this" and away from him. And it was not Mamma who made me want to dance: it was Miss Libby and Minton Lu, not to mention Victor Sylvester. Above all, it was you and the glamorous man-eating mother behind you.

Maureen: After and Before

"Naughty," the nun laughed, "but nice. You've soon found out that she's a chocoholic."

"I knew that sixty years ago."

"Sixty years! Nobody told me you knew her then. She must have been - "

"Ten. Yes. And I was five." He opened the box of Black Magic he had brought and held it before the nun's eyes. "These used to be her favourites. But here - you have first choice. You deserve it."

"Oh no, I really couldn't"

He felt as though he were the serpent tempting Eve.

"Well," he said limply, "it's better than drugs or drink."

"We have plenty of drugs here - and sometimes the liquor gets smuggled in too. Now, where are Maureen's teeth? It's the bane of my life. They're forever getting lost. It's so sad that people who have a sweet tooth end up with false ones."

He hadn't realised that Maureen's were false, since they had been in place on his previous visits. But now she had only just awakened and he could see the denuded gums, the mouth pursed and squashed into puffed cheeks and evidently salivating at sight of the tray of chocolates. She snatched one - it must have been caramel or nougat, for her face registered babyish disgust as her gums clenched against it.

"She'll only be able to manage the soft centres if we don't find her teeth. D' you have any idea where you put them, darling? I know that sounds a daft question, but just occasionally she will surprise us and remember where they are. They're not in your little plastic dish. They're not in your handbag, but I wonder —" the nun swept into the bathroom and came back with one hand dripping water -"no, they're not in the lavatory pan -that's where she stuffed them last time they were missing. We must find them. It's the devil's own business taking her to the dentist, and all hell's let loose when he gets her in his chair and tries to take an impression."

Jack turned his gaze in distaste, from the dripping hand and joined in the search for the teeth, hoping he wouldn't be the one to find them. Going through the top drawer of her dressing table he found something odd. Or rather, something that would have seemed odd to anyone not in the know. It - or, as it turned out, they - were wrapped in yellowing and disintegrating tissue paper. Something bright blue poked out. The something was wrapped inside a flimsy see-'through blouse, once white, now yellowing with the paper. The blue thing turned out to be a pair of wings that a child might wear - diaphanous and suggestive of angels or butterflies. He knew when Maureen had worn these things and who had made them for her. And he thought he knew why Maureen had kept them all these years.

"Are they there?" The nun's voice was sharp, as if meant to jolt him out of his reverie. Maureen was now bawling for the chocolates which had been withdrawn until the teeth could be found. With a prolonged "H'mm" the nun strode to the common room to feel down the upholstery of the chair Maureen usually occupied there.

"The trouble with teeth," she said grimly, "is that even if you do find a pair, you don't always know whose they are. And you can have a nasty accident trying them out." She gave a sigh of much-tried patience. "There's just one outside chance - the laundry."

Jack followed her swift stride into the lower depths of the building, feeling like a small tug tied to a man o' war. Gently she set aside the woman who was yelling obscenities at the notice on the steel door barring it to "unauthorised persons". Jack hesitated, but the nun held the door for him. Stepping inside the laundry was like entering the steam age. It was yet another vision of Purgatory, manned by large strong women, and small weedy men who looked as though smoking in childhood had stunted their growth. All in white, they were dedicated to the act of purification, the patients' sheets endlessly being washed, bleached and sterilised in an atmosphere of vaporous disinfectant and the noise of whirling drums. After a confabulation with the chief strong woman, the nun emerged triumphant with three sets of teeth, explaining on the return journey that,

"They get lost in the bed-clothes and end up in our washing-machines. Not a bad idea, when you think about it, since they get a good clean-up in the process, though they have been known to break, of course."

"You took my chocolates, you greedy bitch," Maureen grumbled when they got back to her. Then she addressed Jack: "That cow took my chocolates - next time you bring them, don't let these buggers see. They're all bloody thieves here."

Unperturbed the nun called out gaily,

"Here are you chocolates, darling. You'll see there's only one gone, and you had it. Now, let's see which teeth are the lovely Maureen's."

To Jack's unsavouring glance the teeth looked more or less alike, and apparently the patients rarely recognised their own, but amazingly the nun seemed to know which were which, and soon the right ones were in Maureen´s mouth and mutilating the chocolate sculptures.

"So, I'll leave you in charge. Will you make sure she doesn't eat the whole lot? She won't want her lunch else - and - well, you know - she's carrying too much weight on her legs as it is."

As Maureen munched, he tried to get her to look into his eyes by crooning another favourite song to her.

"That old black magic has me in its spell,
That old black magic that you weave so well."

But he let his voice tail off to a hum as he came to the line

"And you're the mate that Fate had me created for."

It wouldn't have mattered, though, for she was far more concerned with the chocolates than with his sentiment. When she did speak, her mouth still chomping and frothing with brown saliva, it was to enquire.

"What the bloody' ell are you on about now?"

When he tried to get the box from her, Maureen screeched and clung on to it as if it were her only hold on life. He desisted, sighing and vowing never to bring any more chocolates. Then Maureen's eyes narrowed slyly.

"You can have the chocolates," she said, "if you'll promise to bring me some dynamite."

"Dynamite?"

"You know - I need a good jolloping. I haven't had one for weeks."

Jolloping - he hadn't heard that word for years, it had been a favourite of his mother's. And Mrs Greatbatch's. Perhaps of all the mothers of the Potteries.

"Oh, you'd better ask the doctors for that. They'll have all the proper medicines here."

"They're not a scrap of good. I need dynamite. Senna pods' d do

Maureen: After and Before

the trick, I know it."

"I don't think you can get senna pods now. Besides, you have to steep them overnight. The nuns would see them and take them away."

Maureen's eyes looked even more crafty.

"Well, Choc-Lax then. If you took the wrapper off first, I could keep it in a box like this and they'd think it was just ordinary chocolate. Please. I can't go on like this. I'm all bun up." She lifted her behind as if she were about to show the evidence. So quickly,

"All right," he said.

Snatching one more, she handed him the Black Magic. On the way out he dropped the box in at the office, and enjoyed the sensation of gaining Brownie points when the nun said,

"You've done well, I must say - she usually finishes the lot before you can say Jack Robinson." He did not mention the bargain he had made.

He discreetly delivered the choc-lax on his next visit. On his next visit after that, the nun's welcome was not as warm as before.

"The gerontologist from the hospital is visiting us today and would like a word with you."

Her tone seemed to veil a threat. He gave his weak-joke response.

"Does he want to interview me for admission?"

The nun didn't laugh and, as if holding something back, said,

"The gerontologist is a lady."

So she was, the one Jack had quailed before in the car-park on his first, and what he now wished had been his last, visit. There she sat, formidable, carefully-manicured, wearing the latest fashion in spectacles, clearly on top of her job, a Big Number whose visits were perhaps dreaded. He noticed that the usually cluttered office had been cleared and a vase of freesias brightened the desk and sweetened the air. After formal greetings the lady came immediately to the point.

"I hope you won't mind but I have to ask you this - did you by any chance introduce a laxative into this building?"

His first instinct was to laugh, his second to lie, but the spectacles compelled him to confess:

"Well, yes - Maureen - er - Mrs Devlin asked me to get her."

"I'm sorry. The staff have evidently failed to make you fully aware of the rules here. All the necessary medication is provided. Our work is rendered useless if patients obtain kinds of treatment other than those prescribed. Their very lives can be put at risk."

"What, by taking choc-lax?"

"If we don't know what they are taking."

"But surely they're free agents - they're grown up people who've run their own lives and made their own decisions. I mean, they're not insane, are they? Surely they should have some say in their treatment. Mrs Devlin said your laxatives didn't do the trick."

The doctor looked at him with withering compassion. He felt stupid and sweat-prickled as if he were back at school and about to be punished.

"Would you come with me, please?"

Feeling as though taken by the scruff of the neck and hating himself for his abjectness, he followed her along the corridor and realised that they were making for Maureen's room. Christ, he thought, has the Choc-Lax killed her? But no, Maureen was sitting up in bed looking quite well but with her face turned away and her mouth pouting as if she had been thoroughly chastened. The cleaner was banging the Hoover round more strenuously than usual and looking grim.

"There," said the gerontologis , pointing at the carpet which bore a trail of rubbed-out but still obvious splodges leading to the bathroom.

"Now in here, please."

The bathroom knocked him back with its odour of bleach, disinfectant and something else. The gerontologist pointed at the rubberised flooring, which the last time he saw it was a spotless beige but was now discoloured with smears of brown and black. The cleaning lady came grimly up behind them.

"It must have lain there all night," she said, as if Maureen's turds had been some kind of suppurating corpse. "It's soaked right in. We'll never get those marks out now."

"It is imperative with patients like these that everything is kept as fresh and clean as possible. You can't blame them when there is an accident, but of course if they get outside help...We try to make things as easy as possible for our ancillary staff who are devoted and have a lot to put up with. We must, therefore insist on co-operation from our visitors. However, I freely admit that you are not the first to have done this sort of thing, and I'm sure you won't be the last."

He nodded miserably, as if he had personally messed the floor. He realised that if he argued, he would not be arguing against the woman or even the system but against the process of life itself.

"So, now that that little lesson has been learned, would you like to see the results of Maureen's latest brain-scan?"

"Oh yes," he replied with the enthusiasm of one who has got off lightly. Then he wondered if this meant he was regarded as Maureen's next-of-kin. His visits had never clashed with anybody else's. Come to think of it, there were very few visitors at all and the car-park was usually empty. But of course, if the patients didn't know themselves, let alone friends and relations, what was the point of coming?

Pictures of brain flickered on the computer screen.

"As you see,"- the woman pointed with her felt tip pen – "the brain is under attack from toxic proteins tangled round the nerve-cells and restricting the blood-supply - it's beginning to shrink now under this pressure."

All he saw were streaks and swirls of grey and sepia that might just as well have been negatives of Maureen's faeces. So does the soul shrink with the brain, he wanted to ask. Instead

"But aren't all brains over a certain age shrinking?" he asked. "I'm sure mine is - I dash upstairs to fetch something and forget what it is by the time I reach the landing."

"Well, you're not a patient - " The word "yet" seemed to hover in the air. "And you may not be the type any way. There is a genetic component in all this - if there is a history in your family - well - the chances are that much greater."

"What is so terrible is that the personality can die before the body dies."

"Our patients are not zombies, you know. They constantly surprise us with the remnants of their former selves and even the strength sometimes that the personality shows. I constantly remind the staff, as I remind myself, that these people had full lives just like you and me, they are as human as the rest of us. Only, we're perhaps none of us quite as human as we think we are - what I mean is, we're not as special and unique as we imagine we are. And our control over our own bodies and brains is very limited. The physical processes follow common and well documented patterns."

"So will Maureen's brain shrink dramatically?"

"Eventually it must, but there's no knowing when or by how much. I won't bore you with specialist talk about aneloid proteins and amino-acids. And nothing is gained by using the over-used word Alzheimer's at this stage. We can only wait and watch for the signs."

"But to what purpose if we can't do anything to stop it?"

The doctor sighed at the typical layman's question.

"We can learn to alleviate the effects, we can give whatever treatment is currently available, and, by noting the progress of every case, we may - we shall - find a decelerating drug."

"A postponement of the inevitable?"

"All medical science is that. Our aim must be to help the patient to lead as normal a life as possible."

"And die of something else?"

The woman bent her head in grudging agreement. He felt emboldened and even a slight palpitation in asking.

"Do you believe that Maureen has a soul?"

There was a pause. Then

"I'm a Catholic, so I have to believe it."

"But this breakdown of the personality, of the self - all the research into the brain - doesn't it go against that belief?"

The woman sighed a deeply personal non-professional sigh.

"Sometimes I think so. Certainly to a layman it must seem so. But you know, I came into medicine because of my beliefs. Women can't be priests - oh, I know they can become ministers, preachers - and nuns, of course - but not real priests. When I was a girl, I wished I'd been born a boy so that I could become a priest. Then, when I grew up, I thought if I can't cure souls, I'll cure bodies. But after all the starry-eyed idealism of the student comes the realisation that you can't cure the body of its mortality. However, you can take care of it while it is alive. But to do that effectively, you - or rather, I, one should say - I can't speak for others - have to believe there is an inner essence to each person. The more I am with patients like Maureen, the more I believe in that essence - you may say they have been reduced to it or even purified perhaps, by the chemical process. They are truly themselves, whereas we are still bound up in the projection of our personalities." She indicated her own immaculate turn-out. "I'd hate to think that this is all there is of _me_."

Maureen: After and Before

Maureen: After and Before

Ida Lidgett made the blue wings for you as she had made the blue velvet dress for the Sunday School Anniversary. Her house was an Aladdin's cave of exotic objects, or rather, familiar objects exotically presented: dolls, boxes, baskets, tray-cloths, cushions, lavender bags, tea-cosies, hot water bottle covers, whatever was on the verge of uselessness and could be made so ornamental as to be of even less use. Mrs Lidgett, though she lacked plain domestic skill, had a vivid sense of beauty. She knitted, crocheted, hemstitched, embroidered and petit-pointed. Cheap dolls were transformed into rarities by sequins and satins. Utility work-baskets opened to reveal richnesses of white silk and purple velvet. Ordinary cushion covers became masquerades with figures in rosy bowers. Tea-cosies were knitted crinolines topped by delicate china ladies whose indelicate lower halves I looked for in vain. Mrs Lidgett called you "the daughter I never had" and loved dressing you up, trying on you her theatrical creations, which your mother and I loved to see you in. Especially I recall that dainty fairy-costume, with wings of blue silk, tulle skirt and a white satin bodice. There sat the small grubby bright-eyed woman, surrounded by gold and silver thread, multi-coloured cloth, glass buttons and pearly beads, endlessly producing her exquisite unnecessary artefacts while all around her the house became more and more of a shit-hole, as her husband put it.

She snipped at the material and all her bits simply dropped on the floor and were not cleared up. Every chair was occupied by a doll, staring one out and daring one to sit down. Stuff was piled on the sideboard, and its back mirror made it look doubly laden. There were cabbage leaves and potato peelings rotting among the ash of the fire that was hardly ever lit. Step-ladders leaned against a wall. The dining table cringed under layers of dirty plates which would not be moved till they crashed. Food was trodden into the vivid rag rugs and there was a curious combined odour of new materials and old decadence, and an ambience of soiled loveliness. Maybe Mrs Lidgett, now also soiled, the dirt ingrained in her, had been lovely once, when her husband married her, but she had let herself go and he had given up in despair. He came home from work, either to no dinner at all or to something uneatable: hard potatoes and burnt meat drenched with brown water in which there might be a dead match floating. When she lit the gas Mrs Lidgett let the match fall where it listed.

"If your father came home to that," Mamma said, "he'd murder me."

We kids waited for Mr Lidgett to murder Ida, but he seemed resigned to misery in his quiet pale-ginger way. His eyes were sad and lonely, even though he had two sons. He had tried to make friends of them, but their way of coping was to shrug off both parents. The man returned from the pit like a lodger, to the coldest possible comfort.

There was rarely a meal, more rarely a fire, never a welcome. Either Ida was out visiting the sick and dying, or she was sitting absorbed in some new creation and heedless of his entrance. To all appearances, that is. The observer could not know what tremors might be going on inside her as she swam in her debris like a hard potato in its gravy. We only saw the dead marriage, not the love that had preceded it.

She had been serving in a shoe-shop when Bill met her. She normally only dealt with ladies, but that day a staff absence meant that she had to help with the men's footwear. It was fated. He came in for a pair of brown boots. Ida was the only child of a Methodist preacher on the Central Potteries Circuit. Her mother was a model of cleanliness and godliness, and the three of them lived, a Holy Family, in the neatest terraced house I have ever been in. Both parents were small and exquisite. Mr Payne, who also worked in an insurance office, exquisitely handed over his pay-packet to his wife every Friday, and then each day she exquisitely handed him his bus fare to work, along with a small exquisite sandwich pack. Ida Payne had been brought up to be exquisite too, and had been, as my mother said enviously, "waited on hand and foot". My father said she had been an "immaculate conception", a notion which, though I didn´t know what it meant, I spread throughout the neighbourhood.

Though critical of her, my mother had fellow-feeling for Ida: together they complained that they didn't know what their husbands earned because they never saw their pay-packets and always had to beg for the housekeeping.

"I never realised," Ida told my mother, "that other men were so different from my father."

"And I never knew there were men like your father. My dad was a swine, as most men are."

"He's got another woman, you know."

"Who? Your father? Never!"

"Oh no - my father's a saint - no, I mean my Bill."

Ida always referred to him as my Bill: it went back to their courting days when she sang to him "He's just my Bill, an ordinary guy..."

Ida was in our house a lot. And yours. In fact, she was generally in other people's houses. She ingratiated herself with people, "buying favours" by giving them trinkets, playing their pianos, making outfits for them that could only be worn once, reading their tea-cups, and bringing them the consolations of religion. She foresaw horror for the world but comfort for the individual to whom she was giving the "reading". She not only made pretty objects, she wrote poems and hymns full of uplifting sentiments, and would sing or recite at the slightest encouragement, or even when it was inexplicably witheld. Having been brought up as a Methodist lady, she was a competent musician, and sang in a vibrant contralto that people compared to Muriel Brunskill's. She was generous with her time and gifts. Though no cook she made "a good junket" and delivered it religiously to the sick, one of whom was her own Auntie Mary who suffered from pernicious anaemia brought on, so her niece averred, by grief. Auntie Mary's fiancé had been killed in the Great War. I marvelled at a grief of such duration. Another war had come and other grieving, but Auntie Mary went on as if 1917 were only yesterday. Though she gave none to her husband, Ida gave so much comfort to her aunt as to assure her a place in the Wesleyan paradise. Junket was prescribed for anaemia, and junket Mary got in bland and slithery abundance. It made her already wheyish complexion and blank-eyed gaze even blanker.

Chaotic as her own life was, Ida believed steadfastly in Ultimate Order and joy on the Other Side. And she had the power to make others believe it too, at least while they were in her presence. Her husband called her "a religious maniac": she collected denominations as your mother collected shoes, that is, without discarding the cast-offs. Her current fad was the Longton Spiritualist Church, where she had "made contact with the Other Side". She took Auntie Mary along, hoping to speak to the soldier of 1917. But nothing happened, and it seemed that Bill, who said that "the other side" was baloney, might be right. But one night she and her aunt set up their own séance, with glass and letter-board. Nothing much happened there either, except that somebody kept butting in when Ida was trying hard to get the dead soldier.

"I think you're pushing the glass," Auntie Mary said with a yawn, her enthusiasm waning.

"No, no, look. It's going round on its own."

"By God, if it did, you wouldn't see me for dust!"

"Just keep your finger still, but not pressing. We'll see who's trying to get through."

The glass spelt out WILLIAM and kept on spelling WILLIAM and then, suddenly, MOTHER.

"Well, I'm not a mother, so it must be for you, "Mary said." It would be, of course," she added, a touch of irony mingling with her disappointment. "Who d'you know called William?"

"Only my Bill."

"Well, he's not on the other side - yet."

"No," said Ida, thoughtfully.

"P'raps it's General Booth," Auntie Mary said, not without mischief in her tone. "Or p'raps it's the old Kaiser."

"If it is, he's not saying anything sensible. Why would he call me 'mother'?"

"P'raps it's an unborn child. P'raps that's the only language it knows."

The glass had spelt out a lot of gibberish. Ida gave a shudder.

"We must not go on," she said darkly.

The glass was put away and the board wiped clean. The women did not try again but Ida, ever mindful of signs and portents, switched her religious allegiance to the Salvation Army.

She also switched her loving care from Auntie Mary to Ilse Baumgartner. Washed up on our shores and then far inland by the tide of war, she came from a country that had no shores and whose borders had disappeared any way: Austria. People said, that "she had just got out in time". You said this meant she was an international criminal on the run from the police. Even adults then hardly knew how much worse was the thing she was actually on the run from, and thought she might be some kind of spy because she spoke a deep-throated exotic English like Greta Garbo or Marlene Dietrich. Unfortunately, she didn't look like either of these. If she looked like anybody, I now realise, it was her fellow-Viennese refugee Richard Tauber, whom she adored. She was short and plump and fat-cheeked, as if fed on Sachertorte, and she wore rimless glasses from which black laces hung, so that it looked as though she had a monocle in each eye. We were thrilled by the black cape she flourished as if arriving for a first nights at the State Opera. The only places she arrived at in Stoke-on-Trent were the Police Station, where she reported monthly, and the Post Office where she worked as a sorter and where her fellow-workers got a lot of typically crass British fun out of her battles with the English language. People who knew her laughed at her; people who didn't were suspicious and mistrustful. The police said she was "a funny bugger", but solemnly pronounced her "no Nazzie" as if this had been a possible line of enquiry. Her inner life was a closed book to us, except when a few pages fell out of it during her friendship with Ida Lidgett. You used to love to mimic her.

"You, darling Ida, are my only frient. Only you unterstant."

We wondered what there was to understand. People called her "one of the lucky ones", but what I wondered, was lucky about living in a lodging-house at the top of our street, a place of dim-lit linoed stairways, and smells of gas-metres and falling plaster in built-in cupboards, of old make-up and yellow newspaper linings in dressing-table drawers, of promiscuous smoking and ad hoc cooking?

But at least she had found a friend in Ida Lidgett who really did care for outsiders of all descriptions. She felt at home with and unjudged by them. They appreciated her talents: they admired her colourful and non-utilitarian objects and were more in key than the natives with her aesthetic outlook on life. In gratitude and wonder Ilse spread her red-nailed hands at the sequinned stole and the white satin opera gloves that Ida presented to her. She knew she would never wear them in Stoke-on-Trent, but they conjured up the world she had loved, and nobody but Mrs Lidgett would have thought of that.

Do you have any recollection of the day when, by way of saying thank you, Ilse put a record on her tiny pick-up that was attached by complicated wires to the so-called wireless - the first time I saw this arrangement? The music came out wonderfully loud and clear - too loud and clear judging by the knocks on the wall and the plaster that snickered down.

The reason for the clarity was that both record and pick-up were 'made in Germany', and this guaranteed superiority even though (or perhaps because) the Germans were in league with the Devil. The music was "O Madchen, mein Madchen", sung, of course, by Tauber: so lilting, heady and, in that bodiless pre-war sound, so seductive. I didn't understand the words, but I thought they must be sad because huge tears bulged at Ilse's eyes. She removed her glasses, and the tears moved in slow motion as they fell over her pap-like cheeks.

"I cannot bea-a-arrh it!" she mystified me by exclaiming, as the pick-up arm swished to the centre. "No, no, I cannot bea-a-arrh it."

Maureen: After and Before

band. He appeared small at the street corner and then grew systematically larger and larger as he approached us.

He paused to take in the spectacle.

"What the bloody hell?" Then he gave a harsh and terrible laugh. "Christ almighty, woman, what in the name of decency have you done to yourself? Who do you think you are - Mata bloody Hari? Did you - " he turned to us, the juvenile chorus in the tragedy, " - ever see owt like it in your life?"

We shook our collective choric head, for indeed we didn't.

With which Ida woke from her trance. She looked at Bill, then at us, then at Dennis who had crept back to see, but still kept his distance. She seemed not to know where or who she was.

"Come on," the man grated. "I'll show you what you bloody well look like."

He gripped her elbows and marched her then, up the entry and back into the house. We followed at a discreet distance. You peered in at what followed and retailed it back to the rest of us. He stood her in front of the mirror, made her change back into her ordinary soiled garb and, commanding her to "wipe that muck off" her face, gave it a back-handed push to start the process.

Only in musical comedy, perhaps do women "vamp" their way back into a man's heart when he has lost his desire for her. Only in Ilse's imagination and what it fed on. Perhaps if Ida had had a really good meal ready things might have been different. But love of decoration had betrayed her. There wasn't a scrap of food on the table, only knick-knacks and bits of frippery and the discarded bra.

The Lidgetts separated after that. Ida went to live with Auntie Mary, who made a miraculous recovery from her anaemia as a result. Bill and the boys stayed in the family home, but at the end of the war Bill went to live with his "other woman" who did, after all, exist, just as Ida said she did. The boys joined their mother who, having "pigged up" her aunt's home, now rented one of her own. Bill scrupulously sent her a portion of his wages.

Though war had ended, men still died in pit disasters, and in one of them Bill Lidgett copped it. From the account of a surviving collier, just before he inexplicably stepped over to the point where the black rock collapsed on him, Bill cried out,

"Mother!"

His "other woman", upset because he had not called her name, had at least the satisfaction of believing that he had not called Ida's either. What she did not know, however, was that since the birth of their first boy, Bill had always called Ida "Mother". The ultimate satisfaction, indeed, was Ida's, for she knew that, when Bill called out, he not only called to her but did so in a voice that had tried to communicate once before, and came as clearly now as any voice could, from the Other Side.

Ida Lidgett also made the flimsy blouse – but not for you. It was the first see-through blouse to appear in our unstylish world and was said to be made from "the finest parachute silk", though it must have been nylon. It was made for Edna, the lodger with our next door neighbours (going up the road as you were our neighbours going down). I first saw it on the last New Year's Eve of war-time, and couldn't wait to tell you about it.

The Medwins asked my father to pose as a dark stranger and let the New Year in for them. As my mother called him "a Jekyll-and.Hyde character" this seemed a suitable role for him. Until that night I thought ours was the only household harbouring a Jekyll-and- Hyde.

Jimmy and I were excited to be at a party that would go on after midnight. Apart from him and me and Mamma and Dadda, there were the Medwins, Mrs Medwin's Irish mother, Edna the lodger and Bonzo the bull terrier.

Bonzo's face had a human, rather Slavonic look about it, sympathetic and not at all fierce. Mr Medwin was always urging him to be more assertive, with

"Get that cat!" or

"Goo on, you bugger!"

Bonzo went on but never "got" anything until that night. All he did was wag his tail, or rather his behind, while his grin widened on his wide face. Dadda said that Mr Medwin was "a broken man" since, being a collier and having bought Bonzo as a fighting dog, he had lost face because Bonzo "lacked spunk." Jimmy and I nudged each other at this. It was true that Mr Medwin had a diminished face, since he had had his teeth out and didn't care to wear his dentures. I looked for the "break" in him, but didn't see it till that night.

Despite that lack of spunk, Mr Medwin loved Bonzo. The dog was always there for him when he came home from whatever shift he was on at the pit, and always with the widest grin and the most shining eyes. Which was more than could be said for Mrs M. She, my mother wistfully said, always pleased herself, which is what I foolishly thought all grown-ups did. What especially pleased her and her Irish mother was to go "out and about at all hours" and to "cavort with the Fathers." I wondered how she came to have more than one father, until I saw her and her mother one Saturday afternoon outside the Coachmakers Arms with Father Mahoney and Father O'Shea. There were eight smiling eyes, not quite focusing, in four rosy faces as if bathed in the glow of a Galway sunset, and their unfocused voices were singing 'The Boys of Wexford.' Mrs Medwin was not only, as my mother put it, "very free with the clergy" but also with her husband's wages. He worked at Hanley Deep Pit stripped to his baggy smudged singlet, and when he came home black dust was everywhere. You told me your mother had said that Mr Medwin "smelt of frustration", which I thought was something he picked up at the coal-face. I sniffed round him that New Year's Eve, hoping to find out what frustration smelt like, but he seemed to smell like other men, of sweat and cigarette smoke. Though there were pithead baths, some miners still preferred to be bathed by their wives. However

"I'll not be a valetting service for any man," declared Mrs Medwin, though she lovingly laundered the soutanes and stoles of the Fathers, who perhaps didn't count.

Mrs Medwin was, Mamma said, "in her prime"; in fact, she was never out of it and flashed a fine set of false teeth to prove it. Her mother, Mrs Doherty, was as archetypal as herself, a widow of the Western World whose long-forgotten husband had been a sottish Scot. My father claimed Irish ancestry and, though fiercely anti-clerical, had a fellow-feeling for the indomitable downtrodden. More than that, he liked his drink, and had a repertoire of smut, and was often to be found in the Coachmakers alongside the Doherty ladies and their holy fathers, sending them into fits. On top of a good drink and a good laugh they all liked a good bet, and the others always seemed to do better out of Dadda's tips than he did himself.

So it was only natural that, at her mother's prompting, Mrs Medwin invited him to let in this momentous New Year. Under the diamonds of the last December sky of war-time, Mamma, Jimmy and I crunched diamonds of frost as we passed from our own front door and knocked at Medwins'. Dadda was yet to return home from the afternoon shift at the Steel Works, and Mamma was on tenterhooks lest he got diverted.

"I only hope he hasn't forgotten," she muttered. "When he gets celebrating with his cronies he forgets he's got a family."

It was a house of women we entered. Mr M., having just got home from his shift, was "titivating himself upstairs, would you believe?" said Mrs Doherty. And there, with the two older ladies, was the lovely

Edna Murphy who was married to a soldier on active service with an Ulster regiment. She was keen and dark and challenging. Mrs Medwin often avowed that Edna had "married Brian Murphy and not vicky-verky." I thought Victor Verky must be the name of a disappointed suitor and I felt sorry for him. Mrs Doherty said that Brian "let Edna wear the trousers" — as if there was only one pair available.

However, Edna wore a whole range of trousers, and turbans, and was well known for the way she wore them, standing jutting-hipped, with one hand in a pocket and the other holding up a provocative cigarette.

"She thinks she's Barbara Stanwyck," mused Mrs Medwin.

Edna became even more well-known for the see-through blouse that she wore on extra-special occasions, such as that New Year's Eve. In place of the usual turban there was a peacock-blue ribbon in her dark Drene-scented hair. Jimmy and I couldn't take our eyes off the blouse, or rather, what it both concealed and revealed: elastic straps, metal fasteners and bra cups. And no petticoat! We knew from what Mrs Doherty called "the fillums" that these sights were what excited men, so we were determined to be excited too. I nudged Jimmy every time Edna fished inside the blouse to restore a strap-ribbon to her shoulder, and Jimmy nudged me when, reaching up to take the now out-of-date calendar off the wall, she revealed a little dark fuzz in her arm-pit. I tried very hard to find all this   exciting. How was I to know that the beauty of the blouse lay in mistily displaying arms and shoulders? It took the other women to appreciate Edna's youthful rounded limbs, even though they did so grudgingly. They were not only aware of the girl's beauty, but also of its effect on men. My mother was just this, and Mrs Medwin just the other, side of forty. And forty then meant forty. The old widow saw their predicament with gloating clarity and wry sympathy. She kept making sotto voce comments, but not so sotto as not to be heard by pricked-up ears. Though the remarks were spoken by one woman, they expressed the collective thoughts of three, going (with soft breaths indrawn on the vowels and extra stress on the sibilants to give a more sensual insistence) along the lines of,

"Oh yes, she's a glamour puss and no mistake. And doesn't she know it? You can tell by the way she looks sly under her eyelashes to see if the men are watching her — " (Just then the only men present were Jimmy and me) - "and did you ever see such a thing as that blouse? She might just as well be wearing nothing at all — " (I nudged Jimmy) — "she might just as well be stark naked — " (Jimmy nudged me) — "I tell you, I just dread those men coming in and seeing her, there's no knowing what they'll do when they see that ."

We boys couldn't wait for "those men" to enter. Edna was going to and from the back kitchen fetching mince pies out of the oven, but you could tell she heard what the widow was whispering, for she smiled to herself in an inward, trance-like way.

"Mother of God, will you look at the way she swings her behind round the place. The men'll be after smacking it, you mark my words, and it's just what she wants."

I was amazed to hear that anybody wanted what I did my best to avoid.

"But what can you expect of a Protestant? They're sex-mad, the lot of them."

This was news to me, as conventional wisdom said that sex was a Catholic obsession.

We heard our front door bang to, signifying that Dadda was home. Mamma went to give him his supper and remind him of his midnight task. I watched her go with fear in my heart. Would she find Jekyll or Hyde? Celebration could make Dadda go either way. It might have helped slightly if I'd known which,which. I wished I had gone with her, since I was most afraid when she was alone with him, though, to tell the truth, they could go to bed in an atmosphere of fury and murder and rise in the morning sunny and smiling. I did not know then that Dadda's rage was really against himself, or that women had ways of turning male violence to their own advantage.

I sat in the Medwins' living room where I could press my ear to the wall between it and ours. I had often done this on the other side. It seemed strange and even shocking to be listening in to my own home, almost as shocking as listening in to Lord Haw-Haw. Nothing alarming came through, however, and Mamma returned smiling.

"He says he's ready when you are."

"And doesn't he know," asked Mrs Doherty with a twinkle, "that I'm always ready."

Everybody laughed, except Mr Medwin who, titivated to little effect but smelling of carbolic soap instead of frustration, had joined us now.

"I could have let the New Year in for Christ's sake," he was heard to mutter to Edna.

"Oh no, but you couldn't," his wife declared. "That'd only bring us bad luck. And besides, you're not tall enough or dark enough."

"Strange enough though," the widow tittered behind her hand.

"And what's more," the wife went on, "you haven't a tooth in your head."

"Or a hair on top of it," the mother-in-law capped. Again everybody laughed, except Mr Medwin.

"Well, my dad's bald too," Jimmy said, sensing the man's need of support.

"Balding," Mamma qualified. "He still has enough hair to be the dark stranger."

We stared at Mr Medwin's head with its colourless horseshoe fringe round neck and temples. It was hard to imagine that he had ever been young, harder still to imagine him catching Bernadette Doherty's eye, which was known as a roving one. It had roved all over the place before settling on Arnold Medwin. But though small, he was strong and brave, as his fellow colliers testified, since his job entailed testing the moving cables of the pitshaft lifts. He was to demonstrate his strength that very night. He also had what Mamma later called "a funny look in his eye", particularly as now his eyes had the mascara-like outline typical of the washed miner.

There was a loud knock at the door, and we all went quiet as with religious reverence. All, that is, except Bonzo who barked hollowly.

"It's the Dark Stranger," whispered Mrs Doherty, "and he's knocking fit to wake the dead."

"I'd better go and let him in," Mrs Medwin chuckled, "before he breaks the panels."

The Medwins were proud of the long strips of engraved glass in the top half of their front door. Though the houses were identical in most respects, ours lacked this embellishment.

As the front door opened we heard the All Clear siren, though there had been no air raid. We heard the Stranger and Mrs M. chuckling together, and then there he was, wreathed in beer-breath and smiles, shining-eyed but seeming not to recognise us. He stood with a chunk of coal in his hand, and he spoke in deep organ tones as if he were a priest:

"A Happy New Year to you all."

Then he passed us by without acknowledging anyone in particular and, stumbling through the dark back kitchen, opened the back door. The cold new year's air came through to us. The Stranger's footsteps receded down the back yard.

"He's going to call for a piddle in your lav," Mamma laughed, breaking the spell that had transfixed us.

"I bet he's got a skinful," murmured the widow admiringly, as if this in itself were a sign of manhood.

Her bet was a good one, as we gathered from the length of the interval before he passed through the back gate, down the entry, along the side street and back through the front door.

"He'll be in and out of bed all night," Mamma grumbled.

"If there's any night left," laughed Edna.

I gazed at her, wanting the night never to end. I wished we had a lovely newly married lodger too, not knowing how soon we would have one and that, dear Maureen, it would be you.

When the Stranger re-appeared it was as if discharging the skinful had turned him back into my father, and he knew us after all. I was as relieved in my way as he had been in his. I didn´t really like to think of him as the Dark Stranger and wondered why it pleased the Doherty ladies to do so. He was, it is true, different from other men, "one on his own" as Mamma put it, and I trembled whenever he spoke in public about the Royal Family or the British Empire, without due reverence and patriotic fervour. One neighbour called him "a bloody Nazzie" when he deplored the saturation bombing of German cities. I did so want him to be like other fathers.

Now the party really began. We did the Tarara-bumdeay by way of overture, bouncing our behinds against each other's with abandon. There seemed a special license about this New Year´s Eve. Men would be coming home to reclaim their wives and their wives' jobs; the trousered and turbaned brigade would go back obediently to their skirts and cookers – even Edna, who was at the cooker just at that moment, abstracting goodies that had been made with 'alternative ingredients'. It was hard to imagine that she, so vivacious and full of 'what it takes', would ever be content with the untrousered life. As she bent to the oven, I noticed Mr Medwin's bald head cocked intently forward, his eyes fixed on her haunches. And I heard Widow Doherty stage-whisper,

"Would you look at that fella now?"

It wasn't clear which fellow she meant, for Dadda was also a sight to be seen. He was performing one of his favourite tricks: holding a cigarette in the cleft of his chin to much female mirth. Jimmy and I were not amused: we had seen this feat too often, and it didn't seem much of one any way. However, when Edna came in with steaming sausage rolls and asked what the joke was, Mr Medwin tried to perform the trick just for her. Having no cleft, however, he failed. Mrs Medwin, with a glance of contempt at her husband, called on Dadda to "do it properly." Dadda went one better: he took out his lighter and handed it to Edna, indicating that she should place the fag in his cleft and then light it. For a few seconds he held it there, smoking away all on its own, until

"Ooh, what a waste!" the girl cried and took the cigarette and drew on it ecstatically, at the same time clearing, with a little varnished finger-nail, a strand of tobacco from her dark red lips. Then she handed the fag back to my father who, as he took his drag, held her gaze through the smoke-swirl. The other women were also mesmerised by what they could see through the smoke, and their laughter died. Mr Medwin's eyes took on their 'funny look', while Mamma looked as though she might prefer her man to be in a bad mood if this was what happened in a good.

Normally Dadda and Mr Medwin saw eye to eye on things, especially those that concerned the working man. But about Edna it was eyeball to eyeball. When Dadda, with a neighbourly nudge, said,

"By God, you're a lucky bugger, having a cracker like that about the house," the 'funny look' could have killed.

The hot mush of pastry filled my mouth, and the hot little room became ever hotter as Mrs Doherty stoked the fire with her son-in-law's coal concession.

"Would you look at him now?" she re-iterated, but again nobody knew which him she meant, for both men's eyes were devouring the 'cracker' as our mouths consumed her rolls and pies.

"How about putting a record on the gramophone, Jimmy?" Mrs Medwin suggested, "so's we can have a dance."

Jimmy was the acknowledged doyen of the gramophone. Even before he had learned to read, he had been able to pick out any record asked for. He wound the spring that shared with a great horn the hidden depths of the cabinet. He chose his favourite: 'All the Things you Are.'

Dadda sang some of the words and then ba-ba-ba-boomed the rest, directing it at Edna. Neatly she avoided him and, confronting me, said solemnly:

"May I have this dance?"

I blushed and Edna swung me round. Bonzo danced too, barking happily after his own tail.

"Would you just look at that dog now?" said Mrs Doherty.

Everybody looked at Bonzo – except me. Since it was so close I couldn't help looking at the see-through blouse.

Dadda was dancing with Mrs Medwin whom he kept referring to as "mine hostess." Nobody referred to Mr Medwin as "mine host", or asked him to dance. He looked forlorn. Mamma did a turn with the old widow, who eventually collapsed with puffing laughter, gasping,

"By Jesus, I'm not as young as I was."

"Who is?" Mamma asked.

"Harry is!" Mrs Medwin cried as she whirled past in Dadda's arms.

His vocalisation rose to a climax and his eyes fixed on Edna over his partner's head:

"Some day my happy arms will hold you. ba-ba-ba-boom.

And some day I'll know that moment divine

When all the things you are are mine."

I couldn't understand why I was glad when the swish-swish of the steel needle on smooth shellac ended the song: it had been a pleasure to be in Edna's arms, but I was aware of tension and beginning to find some pleasures too strange and complicated to bear.

"What next?" Jimmy asked.

"What about 'I kiss Your Little Hand, Madame'?" Dadda suggested.

"We haven't got that one," Mrs Medwin said, somewhat peevishly. She clearly saw the way things were tending. "I'm not much for that sort of piffle. But we have got 'Broadway Melody'. "

Jimmy deftly obliged, but, though 'Broadway Melody' happened to be my own favourite, nobody else except me seemed to want to dance to it.

'Embrace Me, My Sweet Embraceable You' restored the romantic atmosphere. This time Edna, again seeming to make a very conscious choice, danced with Mrs Medwin. Dadda had to make do with the old widow, saying,

"Come on, duck!"

"Oh my God, I'm much too old for it."

"Never too old for it – just ask Father Finnegan if you can sin again."

"Ooh, you devil!" The woman went into fits as the devil swung her round, and further fits as he tickled her ear with a smutty joke. From time to time he turned away from her ear to direct phrases of the song at the other dancing couples.

"He's a cheeky bugger, isn't he?" Mrs Medwin laughed. Edna smiled to herself and said nothing.

Did she know that Mr Medwin's haunted eyes were on her all the while?

The lilt of 'I'll Be Loving You Always' drew everyone into the dance, Dadda reverting to his hostess, Mamma getting up with Mr M., the widow with me, and Bonzo with his tail. Edna lured Jimmy away from the turntable, and I saw him trying hard not to look at what stared him in the face.

"Change partners!" Dadda suddenly bawled in an affected tone that made me cringe.

He was standing by Jimmy and Edna. By sleight-of-body, however, Edna managed to grab Mamma, Mrs M. took over Jimmy, and her mother flopped down with a gasp. Bonzo did likewise, I took charge of the gramophone and the two men were left staring at each other.

And though my father barked "Change partners!" several times, Edna went on swinging my mother round the room as if there were no-one else there. Dadda now tried an "Excuse me". But it didn't work. The two women were the best and best-matched dancers, my mother was clearly enjoying Edna's guidance, and their performance drew a round of applause.

"Let's have that again," Dadda said, "only this time it'll be a proper Excuse-Me."

With theatrical gallantry he took his wife in his arms, Edna clutched Jimmy to her, and the Medwins had no option but to dance with each other. Bonzo and the widow sat it out and made encouraging noises.

"Change partners!" Dadda bawled, swiftly snatching Edna from Jimmy and leaving his wife to fend for herself. There was a period of chaos then, out of which Mr Medwin's voice emerged with unsuspected command:

"Change partners!"

He tapped my father on the shoulder just as the music ended.

"Again, again!" the collier yelled, his eyes bulging. I wound the spring and set the waltz on its third revolution.

"For God's sake!" Mrs Doherty fanned herself with her hand. "This tune is getting on my nerves."

At first Dadda would not let Edna go and brushed off Mr Medwin's intrusion with a dry laugh. But then he decided to make a game of it till, with decreasing intervals, both men were calling "Change partners!" simultaneously, and Edna was being hurled from hand to hand like a rugby ball. I, caught up in the frenzy, kept winding the spring and re-setting the needle on the record till the music became unbearable to everybody. As she passed from one to the other, Edna was heard to remark in her laughing whirl,

"What a man!"

Which man she meant and how she meant it became a matter

of subsequent dispute. Edna herself never explained. Each man applied it to himself as expressing wonder at his masculinity. Mamma kept quiet but later said she detected scorn in the tone, and that it must have been meant for Dadda. Mrs Medwin, on the other hand, made an immediate response, bristling with certainty that it showed impudent admiration for her own man.

"So you think he's a man, do you? Well, you should see him in bed – no, on second thoughts you would not want to see him in bed because he's not a bit of use there."

"Shut your trap, woman," the collier shouted, "else I'll black your eye for you."

"Will you listen to the mighty fella talking?" Mrs Doherty appealed to the room.

"And you can clam up, you old bag!" The collier whizzed round on his mother-in-law.

"Is it me now?"

But even Mrs Doherty was abashed by her daughter, who had the bit between her false teeth.

"Yes, Edna, you should see him standing stark naked in front of my dressing-table mirror, admiring himself. Admiring himself! And him no bigger than Wee Georgie Wood and bald as a baby's bottom. And what d'you think he was admiring as he stood there? I'll tell you. It was that long thing and a thankyou that he has dangling between his bandy legs and that he's mighty proud of – though it's no good to man or beast as far as I can tell. So if that's what you want, Edna, you're welcome to it and goo – wa –gh-aagh!"

The voice became a rattle as the small man leapt on his wife, throttling her and yelling,

"I told you to shut your bloody gob!"

And as the man leapt so did the dog. The meek Bonzo had gone mad, gnashing but not quite biting at his master's legs as one in a terrible moral quandary. Foam frothed at his mouth, fear and fury made into substance.

Mr Medwin turned in amazement, and then lashed out at the dog's ribs.

"You bloody coward!" he blasted as Bonzo yelped and backed away from him, his eyes full of a pain that was more than physical.

"Get that man out of here," Mrs Medwin rasped, holding her throat. Her mother and mine rushed to her aid while Edna and Dadda bundled the man – now in a dazed and puppet-like state – out through the back door "for a breath of fresh air" as Edna put it. Bonzo also shot out.

"If that isn't the end of all," whispered the widow.

"It's how I always said it would be." Her daughter shook her head, leaving the 'it' to be interpreted.

"I think," Mamma said, "I'd better take these boys home now."

As we stepped over the front doorstep we met Edna and Dadda calming themselves with a cigarette.

"He'll be all right now," Dadda said quietly. "We shouldn't have provoked him."

"He'll not come back into this house," Mrs Mcdwin called from the passage-way. "I'll not be letting him back in here this night."

"Does she mean Bonzo?" I tearfully asked my mother as she turned the key in the lock of our front door.

"No, she doesn't mean Bonzo. She means Mr Medwin. But she doesn't really mean him either." Mamma was used to final things not being final.

I was re-assured. I could bear to think of Mr Medwin out alone and unhappy in the winter night, but not his dog.

In our house the fire had slumped to ash, and the silver fish were up and doing among the twists of cokernut matting. I thought it would be hard to sleep after all the excitement, and it was already New Year's Day and it seemed a pity to miss a moment of it. But I must have fallen asleep straightaway, as I was wakened by a terrific crash. Jimmy and I leapt out of bed and ran into our parents' room. Dadda was already getting his trousers on and cursing the braces for twisting. He dashed downstairs and out through the front door. Shadowy figures with slit-beam torches went to and fro on the road outside. We saw a police helmet which was both frightening and re-assuring. A car drew up. Voices were raised and lowered and raised again. It seemed ages before my father returned to say,

"It's Arnold Medwin. He's smashed their front door in. They've had to fetch the doctor. There's blood everywhere."

The beautiful glass panels shattered and jagged with Mr Medwin's blood kept presenting themselves to my imagination. It seemed that mild little Mr Medwin was a Jekyll-and-Hyde too, just like Dadda. In their contest of strength the men had exposed their weakness and pathos in front of the women. It was only what women expected and were accustomed to, but for us boys it was not the way we had been taught things should be.

Mamma was right – Mr Medwin was allowed back into the house. I sometimes caught sight of him shambling down the yard to the lavatory. One of his hands was thickly bandaged and for weeks he was on sick pay. He was subjugated, and remained so for the rest of the time we knew him. Sorrow hung about him, but, when I discreetly sniffed around him, I could not smell frustration.

By contrast his wife seemed to expand, cavorting more and more with the Fathers, aided and abetted by the mother. She wrapped a pretty rosary bead-chain round her neck to hide the marks and to remind her husband of his sacrilege against her body.

There was one lasting grief: that night Bonzo had fled from his divided loyalty into the New Year's darkness and the New Year's strangeness. Though Mr Medwin and I called his name for many eves afterwards, he never came back, and the little collier pined for him far more than he ever did for Edna or, it has to be said, for his bold Irish wife.

I could hardly wait to relate these events to you, thinking you would share my anxiety about Bonzo. But what really interested you was the see-through blouse. You couldn't wait to try it on. And trying it on led to borrowing it, and borrowing led to coveting, and coveting to telling lies to keep it.

Maureen: After and *Before*

"She's been a very very naughty girl." The nun greeted him as he passed along the corridor.

Oh Lord, he thought, has Maureen got hold of some more laxatives? Shall I be blamed? Will they be moving her to a secure unit?

But the nun had a twinkle in her eye which suggested something venial. She gave a strange little smile and tapped the side of her nostril.

"She was missing from her bed this morning. You'll never guess where we found her -"

"The mind boggles-"

"In bed with Mr McKendrick."

Jack's mind did boggle.

"Oh, now look at your face! It's not as bad as it sounds. Mr McKendrick is ninety-three and has a pacemaker, so I don't think he'd be up to much - he didn't even know she was in the room. He was sitting watching a football match on his telly, and she crept in behind his back. It was only when he got into bed that he realised he was not alone there. Touching, isn't it? Like Goldilocks. She's done it before - and always on Mr McKendrick."

Jack thought of several comic rejoinders and suppressed them one by one. It was all right for a nun to joke about sex, but you couldn't say anything back that wouldn't sound vulgar or provocative. He saved one up, though, for when he saw Maureen.

"I hear you've been sleeping with strangers."

"Strange what?"

"A strange man."

"Which strange man?"

"Mr McKendrick."

"Mr Mcwho?"

"Sister Gabriella says you got into the wrong bed."

"I certainly did. It stank."

He dared not ask of what, but she seemed to think he had asked.

"That thing you put in your mouth - you know - with a long wotsit." Jack's mind boggled again. "His teeth're black with it - you know, you set a light to it. He sits in bed smoking it, the dirty bugger."

"Oh, you mean his pipe!"

"What did you think I meant? I don't fancy him, you know - not one little bit. He thinks I do but I don't. They say he was manager of Tunstall Co-op, but I don't believe it. The Co-op wouldn't keep a manager who smoked like that."

"Well, it was a long time ago. After all, he is ninety-three."

"Ninety-three? Don't talk so daft. He's thirty-eight and still living with his parents."

Was she confusing past and present here, or confusing two different men? Presumably this was what the medical staff meant when they said she had "lost touch with reality". But was anybody in touch with that? If Maureen was dislocated and freed from time, then for her a man of ninety-three, having been thirty-eight, must, if she had not seen him since, still be thirty-eight. Jack did a quick mental calculation. If Mr McKendrick was born in 1907 he would have been thirty-eight in 1945. It was possible that Maureen had known him then, just possible even that a thirty-eight-year-old man and a sixteen-year-old girl - he cut off his conjecture by suddenly asking her,

"Do you remember how we used to walk to Selham Park when we hadn't enough money to go by bus?" He was immediately annoyed with himself, because the nuns had told him to avoid questions beginning with "Do you remember?" Memories had to be unearthed by cunning and stealth. But

"Yes," Maureen said. "I went there the other day."

Jack's heart skipped a beat.

"So do you remember the Gamekeeper?"

"Me mam took me. There was a man driving the car. She said they were having a wotsit - you know - any way, she said I was sure to win. I didn't though. I fell down."

This was a memory he had no share in - supposing it was a memory and not a fantasy.

But would one fantasize about falling down and losing a contest? No, but one might dream about it. Jack had noticed that often when Maureen appeared to recall something, she was actually remembering a dream. She had not lost touch with her dreams.

"I fell down." She began to cry like a little girl who has hurt herself. He took her hand.

"Come with me now."

"Where to?"

"Selham Park."

"Will you be nice to me? You won't hurt me, will you?"

Her girlish pathos overwhelmed him.

"I would never hurt you."

Fifty years back a girl might have used the word "hurt" as a euphemism for "fuck". Was her pathetic question an <u>invitation</u>? For God's sake, Maureen, he longed to cry, how many men did you say that to when you were a girl?

Maureen: After and Before

Maureen: After and Before

We walked over a railway crossing, by a town-field that fringed the slag-heaps of the Duke's Pits and on to the tow-path of the canal, which ran beside the Trent, one green, one brown cord. The kiln-smoke thinned to a haze; allotments and sewage-farms gave way to crop-acres that had been dug for the "Victory" that was about to come. The smell shifted from human to cow dung. The temperature from town to country was different too, less baking but more prickly and fly-ridden. It was July, and because a boy doesn't take pains to stay in the shade or to move slowly, he becomes part of the heat and for a while revels in it, racing through it as it races through him.

We entered the big fields, and I had never seen such spreads of wheat and barley, moving as one, a tidal wave but more gentle, furling and unfurling with a soft irregular swish. At least they seemed soft when I merely looked at them: it was different when I got among them. These heads were as high as my own. I darted through the thin outer columns and blundered into the golden thicket whose massed ears curved towards me as if to listen more intently to the earth below us. But the stalks became a paling of spikes and spears. I was scourged by stems that sprang back in my face at each tread. At last I stumbled back on to the path.

You were there, looking your calm ordinary self. I was stung all over, my skin was an envelope of sore salt - and you walked on! I caught up with you and pointed at the blood on my arms and legs. From the short sleeve of your frock you drew out a hankie, damped it with your saliva and then wiped away my blood. Immediately the soreness ebbed, confirming my faith in you. You had been there always and it was not possible that we should ever separate. I kept glancing up, as a dog does, and seeing to my doggish satisfaction your gleaming sweat-curly hair in a halo of sun.

We had to toil up a bank lined with the last hedge-roses in all shades between ivory and dusk pink, and all scents from first flush to overblown. Then there were elder-flowers, in spangles green and white, and fox-gloves just opening to admit all sorts of visitors with their various feeling legs and probing noses. The sounds and scents entered the hot magnetic field about my body.

You always annoyed me by insisting on waiting till we reached the top of any hill before you would open our water-bottle.

"Not until then," you said. "It won't be long."

But it always was long. I hated your not-until-thens and kept reminding you of the bottle's existence. But you could be ruthless when you chose, knowing, of course, that the quenching would be all the more ecstatic for the waiting. We watched each other over the bottle, to make sure our swigs were of equal duration. You allowed me an extra glug but took firm hold of the bottle, dragging it from my lips that otherwise would have drained it.

"Save some for the Park - just in case."

"But there's the stream there."

"Well, you never know."

You used the phrases that mothers used.

At last we came to a deer park with woods and hills and drifts of evergreens whose droppings made the path crisp and brown. The park in those days had two very different kinds of inhabitants, one nice, one nasty. We saw the leader of the former first, antlers poised as if he were posing for a clay-modeller. We stopped, would-be statues too. You put your finger to your lips. We watched as the stag bent to graze and then stretched up, ears listening, eyes glistening. When he thought there was no danger he gently pawed at the pine-cones as if invoking spirits. Out of the trees they came, soft, shy, beautiful: his does and their young. He stood with his court about him, and at his signal they all bent to graze for a while in the sunlight, which dappled their already dappled behinds and lit up their white spine-lines and their tails flicking round like propellers at the wrong end. All heads leaned parallel to one another nibbling among the curls of new bracken. It was like coming upon a remote tribe at prayer. The woodland was their temple, lit by sunbeam-slants.

Then a twig went crack under my foot. The herd turned, all Bambi-eyed and twitchy-nosed, and they were off, bounding between tree-trunks, antlers click-clacking, and hooves raising leaf-mould. The glade was suddenly empty, with only the smell of disturbed earth to say who had been there. I felt the forlornness as a landscape inside me.

"Never mind, duck," you said. "We were lucky to see them at all. Any way," - you always had something up your sleeve for consolation - " we can have our first sandwich now. But I'll have t'ave a pee first. Keep an eye open, will you?"

I stationed myself importantly on a mound under a beech-tree. Though I pretended to be craning up at its top branches, the corner of my eye was aware of pink panties being taken down and your head bobbing over a rhododendron bush.

"Quick!" I cried, as if the process could be speeded up. "Somebody's coming."

"Little fibber!"

But for once I wasn't fibbing. The tramp of many feet sounded on the forest-floor, and it wasn't the herd coming back to graze. It was the Nasties! You gave a squawk and rose in a hunch from the bush, obviously pulling up your panties and beating your skirt straight.

A squad of P.O.W.'s came up at the double, carrying picks and shovels instead of rifles against their shoulders.

They were stripped to their waists and looked as brown and vulnerable as the deer. They lived in a set of tin-roofed huts on the edge of the park. Their bronzed bodies shone with sweat. They carried spades, forks, hoes and rakes, and were being drilled and bollocked about by a single native sergeant. He was like a dog who never tires of barking and being officious. A boiled-looking and salt-and-pepper-coloured dog, with a funny clipped squeak for a voice. The orders it issued were incomprehensible even to us who, theoretically at least, shared its language. The man was dressed as if for India, in long khaki shorts, a sweat-brinded shirt and, where there should have been a topee, a beret. His skin was pale smudged with red and his body-hair was ginger and bristly. His squad, on the other band, were soft, glossy and smooth-haired, all shades of pleasant brown from honey to mahogany. Their teeth were bared in a collective grin, and from the collective mouth came a subdued sensual chuckle, immediately silenced by

"Eyeees fe-er-er-runt!"

but while the heads jerked obediently forwards, the eyes and teeth remained switched in our direction, that is yours. You stood, decent now and upright, but as if in a trance, your hand raised to finger curls softly back from your face. You thrust out your chest just as I had seen your mother do, and stood with your other hand on your hip.

You were like the deer, motionless and seeming to test the air, and the men watched you as we had watched, with a breathless gleam. Then they, too, were gone, passing into the trees and history. Again there was silence and the tense aftermath of magic.

"Oh 'eck!" I said. "We've seen <u>them</u>. Now we shall have bad luck."

"That's a lot of piffle. They're only men when you've done."

"Mrs Greatbatch says Gerries should all be shot."

"For your information they're not just Gerries, there're I-ties and other things as well."

I couldn't believe it: my Maureen defending the Enemy! In retaliation I aimed at your soft spot.

"Well, Mamma says they're eating all the deer."

"It's probably all they have to eat, poor things."

I stared. But this was not all.

"They should eat that little monstink who's ordering them about. He thinks he is somebody, he does."

I peered closely at you, you seemed so different all of a sudden. Perhaps you weren't my Maureen after all, perhaps you were a German spy pretending to be her. Perhaps you were leading me to my death! Just like a spy in a film you kept glancing back conspiratorially. I soon realised that you were edging us round the perimeter of the camp where the curved huts stood, alien too, among the fir-trees. One young brown fellow spotted us and gave a low whistle. Others stepped out of doorways, as discreetly as the deer from the trees, and stood gazing at us.

A few sidled up to the wire. One flicked at the hair overhanging his forehead. Another obsessively trained his Mafioso-style moustache. Another drew his hand in circles round his nipples and fingered deep into the hair between them. One, his eyes-lashes meshing, touched his trouser-front with a slow sleepy motion.

"Pretend not to notice," you hissed as we passed by, though you were obviously noticing everything and had deliberately brought us here to do so. Suddenly the squeaky bark was heard, the boiled face appeared, and the bristly arms gestured. You grabbed my hand and scooted off with me.

I still felt uneasy and afraid. But soon you proved yourself my Maureen after all. Beyond a criss-cross of bramble we saw raspberries, like lanterns in the green darkness. As we reached through the barbs and pressed the fruit into our mouths, you became a child again. I got my fingers brambled. You sucked at them greedily, as you sucked at the berries, leaving crimson smudges on my skin. You winked at me as you handed me fruit from the highest branches.

"You know where the best raspberries are, don't you?"

"Yes."

"Shall we go? You dare, daresn't you?"

I nodded, daring anything as long as you led the way. It meant climbing over a spiky wired railing to get into the back end of Selham Gardens, the pleasure-ground that people had to pay to enter. This was trespassing on a grand scale, and risking being caught by a gardener or keeper. Kids had been handed over to the police for it. It gave us palpitations, head-thumping, prickly sweat and tremendous pride and exhilaration. First, we had to climb a hill to where the Gardens' paling made a right angle and so provided extra footholds. A few pines perched high above a sand quarry whose gouged cliffs looked like the edge of doom. Trembling I followed you creeping round the precipice - below was blood-red earth and rock to break one's bones. Worse even than being caught by a keeper was the possibility of being impaled on a railing-spike or tangled in barbed wire like an escaped prisoner.

But you took care of me and everything. You pushed me up to the top bar of the paling and told me to hang on to a spike with both hands. Then you clambered up and over. You lowered me gently, with a little squeeze of complicity. I smelt the sweat of your arm-pits, which I liked. It was the Maureen-smell, an essential part of life.

We crashed through the twilight world of the woodland. Monkey puzzle trees and giant redwoods had been set among the oaks and beeches by forgotten dukes for heirs who were now forgotten too. The present "heirs", the paying public, never got this far into the Gardens.

It was a secret world which only the long-dead, and a few of the living, such as ourselves, knew. It was not a silent world, though: its noises hollowed out and gave dimension to the silence around us. Even the birds hardly dared to speak in this perpetual dusk. Sunlit breath slanted between the sheer fir-trunks, breath of wood and resin, breath of fern, fungus and leaf-mould. Branches snagged at us, but also stretched out their hands to help us up the slopes. We were rounding the lip of the basin into which one end of the lake was fitted, and we could see its water twinkling below.

"Don't slip, else you'll roll in and be drownded," you warned, making me afraid I was going to slip at every step. There would be nobody down there to save me. The pleasure boats all stayed up at the safe end of the lake where it met an ornamental esplanade. We could not see the Gardens because the old dukes had let the distant woods grow thick to blot out plebeian intrusions in the views from the mansion. The intruders, of course, had eventually taken over, but you would not have known it from here. The woods had been the breeding-ground of the pheasants and deer which generations of aristocrats had come here to slaughter. If birds and animals had ghosts, multitudes of them must have been haunting these woods.

We found a few more raspberries, but they were too hard and tart.

"They don't get enough sun," was your authoritative verdict as you spat out one after another. You gazed across at a far hill-side which was only very sparsely wooded. "We shall have to go up there."

So down we went into the dip and up again on the other side. Yanked by briars, scratched by thorns, in a nimbus of gnats and sweat, we made it panting to the sun-kissed bushes. There the berries offered themselves like fat pink caterpillars to our pink fingers, and crushed sweetly on our eager tongues.

"We must save some for later," you said. I knew you would. You laid your handkerchief open on the grass to receive whatever offerings our mouths could spare.

So feverish were we to get our fill that we did not at first notice the figure looking down on us. Being on the summit, it had been hidden by the hill's convexity. But as we wove upwards, like ant-eaters with noses to the ground, it reared over us. Suddenly I saw it and gave a screech.

"Whatever's up - oh, it's only the Monument."

"The Monument" was what everybody called it when they spotted it from the Gardens below as the culmination of the designed prospect across the lake.

"It's so big," I cried. "And it's a man!"

It was a statue on a large plinth.

"Well, he won't eat you, duck. He's dead."

But he seemed to me alive. And he seemed to be saying. "I am the Master here."

As the first Duke he had indeed been precisely that. Every time I plucked a raspberry I felt that he registered the theft.

"Forgive us our trespasses." I said.

"That statue's really bothering you, i'n't it, duck?"

"It seems funny being up here, away from everything."

"What - him or us?"

"Him - and us."

"It's so as his family could see him from a long way off."

"And so's he could watch them - and us."

"Only he's dead, isn't he? He can't hurt you."

"I know, but - "

"Come on, let's go up to him. Then you'll see he's 'armless."

"H-harmless," I corrected you. "I can see his arms."

"Alright, clever dick!"

We toiled up the last furlong of the slope to its summit, which was bare save for the colossus, shining dully as if with sweat. The bronze man was dark brown with streaks of green as if made of old meat. In order to look at him we had to make his head blot out the sun for us. We saw his beard and staring eyes, his frock coat crumbled by a century of weather.

"See what they wrote about him when he died." You spoke as if the writing would prove that he was well and truly gone.

But we could not read it. There were lots of C's and X's.

"What does it mean?"

"How should I know?" you said. "I don't know everything, you know."

"Yes," I agreed. We looked at each other as if something had been revealed that we didn't want to face up to.

Then you re-asserted your authority.

"If you climb on to that stone and hold the man's hand - "

"Oh I dunna want 'old his hand - it might come alive."

"Dunna be daft. He's not a vampire, you know. Now, put your foot here, and I'll hold on to your legs. Then you'll be able to see what he sees."

I mounted the overlap of the plinth and stood, wobbling at first but then, steadied by your warm grasp, triumphant.

I saw: the pattern, the Master Plan, the image of the mind that planned. I saw Order and Beauty and, though I did not understand what I saw, I knew that something in me reached out to it. First there was the lake in its full length, held cupped at one end by the hanging woods, and in a broad level at the other by the esplanade of the Italian Gardens, whose name made me wonder if the P.O.W's ever walked in them and felt at home there. I had walked in them myself with my parents, and I knew the rose-walks, the pergolas, the urns and statues (of gods and naiads, so different from this stern Duke), but now I saw them in miniature. The people were miniature too, moving as on a chess board.

Behind the Gardens were the remains of the mansion: a tower, a colonnade, stables, a ceremonial port-cochere. But beyond that, something had gone wrong. For there lay the disfigurement we called our home-town, pointed by the cone-shapes of the Duke's own collieries. However, my eye was held by something else, also a misfit in the Master's Plan: a radiant aquamarine rectangle with a white trim in the middle of the woods. The streamlined swimming pool had been built when the Gardens became a people's park. When I pointed it out to you, your face assumed the trance-like look it had worn towards the P.O.W's. I too became dreamy as I thought of the fortunate drinkers in the open-air cafeteria, watching from their white balconies the lithe brown swimmers flexing themselves on the three-tiered diving-board and swooping into the expansive and expensive blue water. It was the life everybody surely longed for – "when the war is over."

We stood for a few minutes at a loss what to do next. But you were never at a loss for long.

"We can cool off in the brook."

I was glad to head downhill again, away from this forbidding sanctum.

We wrenched through briars to reach the point where the stream fed the lake, running shallow over perfect pebbles, the water swirling and bubbling and ricocheting in delicious spray-shoots. It was as if we were the very first people to have come here. Yet there was a plank laid to join the banks of the stream, and it was on this plank, dry and grainy and tar-warm, that you put your frock and I my shirt and shorts, and both of us our sandals. Stripped to our underwear we lowered ourselves from the plank into the stony brook, our widening eyes signalling the onset of the heavenly agonising chill that crept between toes and up ankles. The coldness reached right into my sinus and lifted the hair from my scalp. We squealed in our abandonment to it, not knowing whether we were experiencing pleasure or pain but sure it was ecstasy. We pulled faces at one another and then started kicking the water up, causing the big drops to ping on us like grapeshot.

It was some time before we became aware of being watched. When we turned our backs on each other in a rude version of "Hands, Knees and Bumps-a-daisy" and were almost hysterical, we saw this man standing on the slope above us. He was so still that the glare of the sun made it seem as though the old duke had stepped off his plinth and stomped down the hill after us. Our laughter died on our lips.

The man moved closer. He wore hard leather boots and leggings. His head was cropped close like a German soldier's. We saw the gun and the bag slung over his shoulder. I thought the Enemy had got us. But his voice was not that of a foreigner.

"What the bloody 'ell dost think tha'rt playin' at?"

"Nothing," you replied, and I was awe-struck by your coolness. You sounded just like you mother when confronted by a landlord or clubman demanding arrears. "We're minding our own business."

"Well, tha cost ger ite of that bloody watter. This is private prop'ty, and it's not for any bugger to trespass on."

"Hark at him!" You nudged me. "Lord Muck."

"What dost sey?"

"I wasn't speaking to you."

"Ey, ey, less of thy chilp."

The man came closer, strutting and creaking in his leather. He wasn't old. He was sunburnt, tall and erect as the pine-trees.

"Tha'dst berrer geroff this land quick else I'll hand you over to the Estates Manager."

It sounded terrifying to me, but you only shrugged. I splashed my way out of the water and was about to climb on to the plank when the man's boots trod next to my fingers. He stood over our clothes like a dog showing its teeth. The plank dipped springily under his weight.

"Dost hear me?" the man yelled, but you showed no sign of moving out of the stream.

"I can't come out," you said, "unless you turn your back."

The man's eyes crinkled. I think he was trying not to smile.

"Cheeky little sod," he said quietly, as if pondering the matter.

Then his narrowed eyes caught sight of the raspberries oozing into your rag.

"Been stealing, hast?"

"They are wild. They're not yours."

"They've been picked on this estate. It's a matter for the police, I'd say."

You were trembling now but kept up the act.

"I don't see any policemen round here."

"Oh no? Well, I'm the police on this estate."

Your shrug, I could see, was not really casual. For what seemed a long time we looked at each other - or rather, you and the man looked at each other, and I looked at you. The man seemed to be considering something deep inside himself.

"Or if tha likest," he offered in the drawl of authority making a magnanimous concession, "tha cost tak' thy punishment 'ere and now."

He let his smile show. Yet the smile seemed more threatening than the scowl.

What you said then took my breath away.

"O.K.," you said without consulting me. It was what one always did at school: given the choice between detention and the stick, one chose the stick to get it over with. But this was different. We had no idea what we were letting ourselves in for. Or, to be precise, I didn't. You rose from the water and stood, though frockless, as proudly and dreamily as you had stood before the P.O.W's, one hand on your hip, the other teasing the stray curls at your temples.

The man suddenly lifted me up and, crouching, bent me over his knee. He gave me several sharpish smacks on my buttocks. I felt my groin writhe against his rough trouser-leg and smelt the leather and moleskin smell of him. He smacked until I had the wit to cry. It had not really been painful, but the crying satisfied him. He set me on my feet again and I tenderly fingered my trouser behind. The man winked at me as he turned to you.

"You next." His tone was gentle, almost affectionate.

Again my Maureen became a total stranger to me, as like an automaton you took my place over the man's knee. But it seemed to me not fair because he didn't really smack you. Instead he started kneading your buttocks as if they were clay or dough, and all the while he stared out into space communing with something beyond. You did not resist. I bent down to look into your face and it had the same faraway look on it as the man's had. I was frightened of you both. Suddenly he gave a shudder as if he were having a fit, and he cried out,

"God Almighty!" His legs shot straight out and you rolled off him on to the grass.

And you smiled. You knew. You knew what it was all about. You knew that it was because of you. And I was outside of it and didn't know. The man buttoned himself up.

"Take your raspberries and skedaddle," he said in a crackly voice.

But it was he who skedaddled like a scared fox. You slowly put on your frock and sandals. You unloosed your hair and, prising the clip apart with your teeth, re-arranged it with dreamy deliberation, your eyes fixed on the man's retreating figure. Halfway up the hillside he turned round, his gun pointing down into the earth. You took my hand and we walked, not hurrying, to the woodland path. I glanced back. The man was at the top of the hill with the Monument behind him and the sun behind the Monument. In my mind they merged: the master who had planned the park and the man who policed it. They thought they had us in their power. But, with my hand in yours, and you so wholly self-possessed, I knew otherwise.

"Twasn't me."

He was pulled up sharp. He had thought she was somnolent as usual, not really listening. She had never challenged his previous narratives. He had accepted the idea that he was talking to himself all the while. What was she saying? That he had been in Selham Park with somebody else, or that it hadn't happened at all? He had to move carefully, as the nuns had taught him, not to challenge her but simply repeat what she said with a tone inviting expansion.

"It wasn't you?"

"It wasn't me he wanted,"

His relief in her confirmation of the happening was swiftly overtaken by a kind of fear. He would have preferred not to pursue the matter.

"He?"

"You know - that what-d' you-call-it?"

"Gamekeeper?"

"Gamekeeper!" she laughed as if turning the word over in her mind. "It wasn't me he was after."

"After?"

"Fancied. It was that boy."

"Boy?"

He longed to say "Do you mean me?" but he dared not in case it broke this unprecedented continuity of recollection. He had learned that she needed to separate others from their past as she had herself been separated.

"That Jack."

"Jack!" He repeated the name as if it were someone else´s.

Surely he wouldn't have forgotten that - if it were true? He could see the scene so clearly - had he constructed it as he wanted it to be? Or had she? He felt weak and defeated. The accuracy of his recollection and the way he had read his life had always been most important to him.

"I know men," she pursued, tapping a finger on her nostril "That's how they are."

Had she simply misread the incident according to her own view of things? But what of me then, he asked himself. Do all past events therefore only have a subjective existence and no substantive reality? Do all mirrors distort? He wished he could leave right now and never return. He wished he had not been born. It seemed he knew nothing. Life was totally mysterious and opaque, the memory of it an illusion, and there was no point in trying to record it.

Maureen's in therapy."

"Oh - well, I'll come back another time."

"I'm sure the therapist won't mind you joining in."

"Therapy? I hope I haven't reached that stage."

"It's good for patients to see their visitors as like themselves - not aliens from outer space."

A good idea in principle, he agreed, but as always he was fearful of being involved. However, he meekly followed the nun into what she said, rather wistfully,

"Was once our sewing room where we mended sheets, knitted and darned socks and indulged in a bit of harmless gossip."

No needles clacked away now, and the babble was not gossip.

"The activities are designed to make them feel they are still autonomous human beings - as far as that is possible."

The nun dematerialised, leaving him in the care of the therapist, a short plump woman with crinkly hair almost as long as herself and hardly distinguishable from her draped clothing.

"I'm Lois," she said, pushing back the crinkles.

It was remarkable how many people one met in the year 2000 looked as though they had chosen to remain in 1970. But this woman would have been at most a small child then. Now she was exercising admirable control over a wide range of potentially anarchic activities. It was for all the world like an infant class-room, the patients in brightly-coloured smocks and burbling in concentration as their teacher bustled about from group to group while two orderlies kept their eyes skinned for danger. Some patients were helping to make tea, though kept away from the kettle; some rolling pastry for the oven though the ovens were elsewhere. Some sorted out, as in a nursery school, coloured shapes, large plastic numbers and letters. Maureen's group was engaged in "creativity" with paints and plasticine.

"Your friend Jack has come to join us," Lois murmured in Maureen's ear. Maureen did not look up and, though he sat down beside her, she went on rolling her plasticine into something like a primitive Earth Goddess. As she worked on it, Maureen murmured a mantra:

"Belly, bottom and tits. Belly, bottom and tits. Belly, bottom and tits." When she was satisfied, she held up the finished product and announced, with a cheeky smile to the therapist,

"This's you."

"Oh Maureen. I'm flattered. It's really really good."

But hardly flattering, Jack wanted to add. Again he was reminded of a class-room and a student teacher's longing to please set against the child's desire to hurt. Maureen's smile had been one of conscious malice, and malice remained without a smile as she suddenly squashed the goddess flat with her fist.

"Would you like to do some painting now?" Lois carefully rearranged the plasticine and put it into its container. She set paper and some poster colours before Maureen.

"No."

"Oh, but Jack would like to see your painting - here's one you did last week. It's really really good."

It was too: a small water-colour of rosebuds, pansies and forget-me-not, sharply realistic, even exquisite. Jack recalled that at school Art and Games were the only things Maureen had excelled in. On leaving she had worked briefly as a paintress in a pot-bank till Cara got her a job at the Odeon. Could the skills of eye and hand have remained, after so much else had gone?

"Is this really by Maureen?" he asked, then turned to congratulate the painter herself. "It's marvellous!"

"Of course it's by Maureen," the therapist smiled. "I can show you others."

It was a good job she could, because Maureen tore the painting from her and dashed a brush, dripping with yellow, across its flowers, the hairs making a massive obliterating dandelion head.

"Oh dear," Jack cried. "why did you do that? It was so perfect. I'd like to have taken it home with me."

"One has to be so careful about praising them," Lois murmured.

"If you overdo it, they think you're patronising them, treating them like kids. If they're good at anything, they prefer criticism to praise. They want their successes to be real just as you or I do. In fact there is no 'they' and 'we': they are we."

"What are you whispering about, you fat cow?"

"This gentleman came to see you."

"Who? Him? He's no bloody gentleman. His mam's an underglaze paintress like me, and his dad's traffic foreman at the steel works."

"That's amazing." Jack said. "She's spot on - only half a century out of date."

He wished he could leave now, but he had to submit to the therapist's direction.

"Maureen loves sitting for a likeness. Would you like to try your hand at a sketch?"

"Oh no. It wouldn't be a likeness, I assure you."

"I hope you won't think I'_m_ being patronising when I say it's the activity that matters here, not the end-product. I have to say this to all our visitors - and keep reminding myself for that matter. It was a lesson it took me some time to learn. I can tell you. My training was in Art School, where that word "art" sets up such unrealistic expectations. Art in therapy is just one way of enabling our patients to find thing in themselves that could easily be lost forever. They constantly surprise us with their skills."

"I doubt whether I'll surprise you with mine. But here goes -"

He sat down at the drawing board across the table from Maureen. As soon as she became aware that she was being drawn, she settled into a smiling seductive trance, as if regarding herself in a mirror.

"She just loves having her picture taken," the therapist whispered. "She's like a film star making love to the camera."

"She should have been in show business, as her mother always said."

Maureen's dimpled smile assumed a professional glaze and she sat, happy to be quite still as long as he glanced up from drawing to study her features. But when he had finished she jumped up and knocked paints and brushes flying to have a peek. She put her arm round his shoulder and put her face close to his so that he smelt her hair and breath. It was so like and so unlike the closeness of sixty years back that he could have cried.

"Is that me?" She snatched the drawing.

"Well, it's a sketch of you."

She pored over it, breathing heavily. Useless to tell the patients that the activity was all that mattered: they were only interested in the finished artefact. There was, in fact, no likeness at all. He had deliberately drawn an idealized female face like an illustration for a woman's magazine of the 1950's. She could not possibly recognise herself in it. Yet she scrutinized it as if checking every detail.

"H'm- makes me look a bit old I must say."

Despite her criticism she set the drawing up against a pile of books and kept glancing at it and nodding approvingly. Jack smiled and had to acknowledge that, when away from a mirror, he too saw himself as a twenty-five-year-old.

"Well, *you* seem to have pleased her," Lois, returning to the table, said wistfully. "She always hates my portraits of her."

"That must be because yours are good likenesses. I told you I was hopeless."

"Would you like to take a look at what the others are doing while I get Maureen started on something else?"

The man next to Maureen had a thin moustache on his sad intelligent-looking face. He had created a very presentable landscape.

"Is it from memory?" Jack inquired.

"No, it's from the stepping stones in Dovedale," the man said without apparent irony.

"Then it is from memory, not imagination."

"Memory, imagination." The man repeated the words as if they belonged to a foreign language.

"It's certainly like Dovedale as I remember it." Except that there was something that looked like a short fat woman floundering in the river.

The man didn't actually say "so what?" but he did shrug as if he thought he was conversing with a moron.

"George paints the same picture every time," Lois called as she bustled up. "Don't you, lovey?" Did she deliberately ignore the floundering female?

"No," George said. "They're the same place at different times of day."

"He's got a point there." So it must have been a persistent memory, like a recurring dream. The patients had perhaps not so much lost their memories as lost the knack of processing them in the approved manner.

Lois edged Jack to the table where two men were kneading wet clay and then hugely enjoying thudding it out on the board. A third had got bored with working it into routine pots and was now creating what was obviously an erect cock rising out of a large scrotum. He gave smirking sidelong glances at the others when the therapist came up with Jack.

"Alan used to produce moulds for Royal Doulton," she said.

"I didn't know that Royal Doulton made that sort of thing."

"Perhaps they'd do more business if they did. He's retained his skill amazingly."

It was true: Alan had included all the details, veins and swellings, and, though the balls were large, the whole piece was well-proportioned, not a caricature.

At the next table another trio collaborated on a collage of belching bottle-ovens in stark black and white.

"Now," said Jack, "that really does have to be from memory - all that's gone now."

"Actually," the therapist crept irritatingly up behind him again, "It's from this plastic bag."

She exhibited the original: underneath it read: <u>Gladstone Pottery Museum.</u>

"I should have known - being something of a museum piece myself. But at least it shows that they can still work together."

"Well, yes - they're not exactly autistic, you know - I'm sorry to keep reminding you, but they have been just like you and me, and in most respects still are."

He felt suitably rebuked: it was all too true. Maureen and he had once shared so much, been so alike in so many ways, and, despite the long separation, he still felt his kinship with her. Suddenly he thought that he did not want to lose her again.

At that moment a minor disturbance erupted in Maureen's corner of the room.

"Oh my God!" Lois cried. "I asked George if he'd like to paint Maureen - only I didn't mean it literally."

She shot to where Maureen was sitting with her smock and blouse lifted right up to neck level and her breasts were as proudly on display as the breasts of a seventy-year-old could be. George was dabbing meticulously at them with his brush: having vermilioned the nipples, he was now lovingly covering the corollas with a soft brown and already had a white and pink wash ready for the rest. It was extremely sensual and, in a way, cleverly thought out. The other patients were gathering round and either laughing helplessly or making crude suggestions. Maureen was, as they say, having a ball, her dimples coming and going in rapid succession.

Again Lois showed her admirable aplomb. Waving away the orderly,

"That's really gorgeous," she said. "But I think it's time for tea."

At which there was a general rush to clear up the tables, and poor Maureen was left looking forlorn as even George abandoned her.

"I see," said Jack, "that they've got their priorities right."

"Yes," Lois puffed, as she struggled to clean Maureen up and lower her blouse, "mention of a meal can always be guaranteed to defuse a situation."

Maureen: After and Before

Adrian Ash should have been at a prep school along with others so christened. Instead his mother brought him to Saint Chad's Elementary School where the other kids branded him a 'cissie'. He appeared on winter mornings, not in a home-knitted balaclava such as the rest of us wore, but in a brown leather motoring cap with flaps that popped open and shut by press-stud. He also wore brown leggings and looked like Amy Johnson about to climb into her cockpit. With his fair wavy hair, delicately cut features and nice manners, Adrian became an instant teachers' pet. He sported an oblong wristwatch which, even if it had been boringly circular, would have made him unique in that school. But the main thing about Adrian was that he was a very talented musician, with a superb soprano voice.

He was all of a piece with the world he inhabited, a world carefully constructed around him by his doting parents and idolatrous maiden aunt. They all four lived together in a superior bay-windowed house in the upper part of town, close to the parish church and away from the pot-banks. The Ashes were genteel from their toenails to their hair-ends. They singled me out as the one suitable companion for their spoiled little angel, and I was glad I had not laughed openly at the leggings. I fell instantly in love with the Ashes' world: it was like walking into a "Just William" book. What others called "parlour" the Ashes called "front sitting room" and whereas we lived in our kitchens, the Ashes only cooked in theirs. What was more, they had a "music room". The furniture was mahogany and there were circular ruched satin cushions. Music rooms became as important in my life as they were in Adrian's. Likewise the Established Church, of which naturally the Ashes were pillars. Such people should all have got MBE's, for that is what they were: members of a still intact empire, believing the right things, possessing the right things, doing everything properly, beacons to those of us who hovered only on the margin and had to make do with what came to hand.

Mr Ash was a breezy handsome man with a ruddy face, carefully waved hair, a posh voice and long signet ringed fingers. Being 'in management' he was always seen in a suit, collar and tie, and dark brown suede shoes. He seemed to me just the sort of father one should have. He drove a Riley, and I savoured its petrol odours in winter and hot leather upholstery smells in summer. He sometimes sat me between his pinstriped thighs in the driving seat and laughed at my legs straining, and failing, to reach the controls. I liked the haze of spirituous breath and brilliantine he enveloped me in. The Riley took us to the Ashes' caravan, parked in a farmer's field overlooking Alton's Towers long before they were given over to the leisure industry. It was a scene of perfect beauty: misty Gothic pinnacles touching the blue sky, the crowded warp and weft of pale green fields and dark green woodland, and, bringing up the rear, the wind-scalped Weaver Hills. The caravan was a real gipsy one, curvaceous, painted and inviting as the buttercup field it solitarily occupied. Under its window, stood a huge water butt from whose magical sky-gleamed coolness we drew a bowlful to wash our hands in before tea. The soft water and the soap, a Lifebuoy sliver, its smell mingling with those of bluebells and beech leaves, fixed the scene forever in my soul.

Adrian also had proper birthday parties. There was chocolate blancmange - the very words seemed good enough to eat, even though war restrictions made it taste like a mousse of brown paper - and fairy cakes. One year Adrian wrote a play to perform before his parents and aunt. Naturally, Adrian was his own hero, his cousin Penny was the heroine, and I was happy to play the villain, the smallest villain there ever was. Perhaps it was typecasting, since I had already played Rumpelstiltskin at school. Adrian, routinely given first choice, had refused the role: he would not play any part but that of a handsome prince, being, as he was, a budding Anton Dolin. We had seen Anton Dolin in Where the Rainbow Ends at the Theatre Royal, and become obsessed with the silver saintly knight who saves England. Adrian's play cast him in such a role, and he rescued his cousin from my tiny Hitlerian clutches.

In fact it was Adrian's clutches she found herself in whenever she followed us, as she automatically did, to the garden shed. Adrian was always anxious to see what other people, especially girls, had got, and wasn't averse to incest when necessary. Penny wasn't averse either, and readily displayed what she hadn't got. But when I refused to show the little I had, Adrian cried angry tears and stamped about. It wasn't that I was prudish: I only wanted to show myself to people who aroused me, and neither Adrian nor Penny did.

The shed, like everything belonging to the Ashes, was well appointed. From the window we could survey an overgrown piece of land next door, where a carter from the local fruit and vegetable market parked his horse and dray after a morning's work. When the horse was uncoupled it would pee at great length, creating a hissing steam. Then the swarthy swearing carter unbuttoned himself and – unaware of the two little boys eagerly observing the twin jets - peed alongside his animal. The nasturtiums in their stone urns, the little tufted roses twined round the trellised arch, and the marigolds and snapdragons of the garden became a suffusion of timeless sunlight.

Then we would dash indoors to listen to "The Robinson Family" on the wireless. The Ashes aspired to be like the Robinsons and I aspired to be like the Ashes. But there were conflicts. One Boxing Day Mamma and Jimmy came to fetch me home from a party at the Ashes. Because they had snow on their shoes, they were made to stand in the windy porch whilst I was fetched from the warmth and laughter within. How dim and dowdy they looked in comparison with the bright party-frocked people I was leaving behind. I wanted to stay. It was the first time I had seen a Christmas tree lit by electric fairy lights in an otherwise dark room. It stood beside Adrian's piano, and the smell of hot pine needles became the very breath of the music heard there.

Though it was not the first time I played Musical Chairs and Postman's Knock, it was the first time I played them in so courtly and stylish a manner, with dainty well-spoken guests. And for the first time in my life, too, I received a present from someone outside the family circle: a little press-studded purse that opened to reveal two rough suede compartments smelling of newness and hoarded wealth. In one of them gleamed a spon new sixpenny piece, which seemed much more valuable than the two lumpy threepenny-bits that Jimmy had hung for me in a discarded pill carton on the unlit cotton wool-dabbed tree at home.

As well as the garden shed Adrian had use of the box room: it was his "lab". His parents bought him a chemistry set, with test tubes, litmus paper and lurid crystals in glass-stoppered jars. He graduated beyond toy kits, and soon we were regularly visiting an old-world apothecary, who sold beautiful pieces of clear glass equipment: retorts, beakers, pipettes, flasks conical and spherical, and various sulphates, phosphates and chlorides which came, as if in strictest confidence, by the scruple. Mr Corbishley was scrupulous and cadaverous, creepy and Dr Frankenstein-like in his white overall and half-spectacles. Adrian, of course, had better and more equipment than I: a Bunsen burner instead of a mere spirit lamp, and a real pestle and mortar instead of a large pebble in an old stoneware dish. But I could whip up equally obnoxious abscess-like concoctions and produce equally colourful crystals from a saturated solution. What I couldn't produce at that stage was sperm. Adrian had just started doing so. The sperm did nothing for the litmus paper, so he carefully dribbled it into a test tube and heated it over his Bunsen, all, as he put it, "in the interests of Science". Though nothing significant happened - merely a little bubbling followed by vaporisation and a tiny white deposit - I was impressed, especially when

"I need," he said professorially, "to examine it under the microscope."

A microscope duly appeared, bought by Adrian's Auntie Muriel with much prophetic solemnity about Adrian's "career". Only he and I knew what was to be examined under it.

"Boys will be boys," Auntie Muriel said, more aptly than she knew, her head lovingly inclining and her eyes shining behind her pre-war octagonal spectacles. She perhaps would have liked two boys of her own, but, being pre-war like her glasses, and having a hair-do designed in 1931 and never afterwards altered, she had to make do with her brother-in-law and nephew.

Despite looking girlish, Adrian was a real boy, always exploring new ways of self-gratification and, to be fair, extending them to his bosom friend. But his normally gratified existence was thrown into confusion by your blossoming bosom, dear Maureen. By now you were in the Senior Girls' class, and your seniority was visible before one's eyes. You were already at fourteen what my mother called "a well built girl". We were mere Juniors, I nine and Adrian ten. But it wasn't only the few months between us that made the difference. Ever immature, I only saw faces. But Adrian had become fixated on girls' bodies especially yours. And now, when he heard that you and I were next door neighbours, he, for once, had reason to envy me as I envied him. You became a daily obsession, always referred to in code as IT, of whom the most fleeting glimpse in the playground gave Adrian an orgasmic ecstasy and me the pride a Madame must feel in keeping a well-ordered brothel. Even if you could remember anything, you would not remember this, as it was a secret kept between Adrian and me alone. I must admit I was perplexed by my friend. Whenever I contrived an encounter between you, the self-possessed leader-in-the-making would stand there dumb, writhing with self consciousness, and you would give a shrug which made your budding breast tauten under your blouse, thus tying Adrian's tongue all the tighter. He became asthmatically breathless, and only able to express his love surreptitiously. Around the school there appeared pretty drawings of hearts with arrows dividing the initials "M" and "A". The Senior Mistress investigated, or tried to, but, though we kids all knew the artist, we just looked at her with hard eyes and pursed mouths, since it was none of her business. Our own teacher, the beloved Mrs Nicholas, was far too wise to make anything of it. Instead, she drew Adrian and me further together by making us room monitors, and by conspiring with the headmaster, the vicar and the organist to get us into the parish church choir.

Adrian had always resisted joining the choir, partly because his father was a leading tenor in it and partly from some unexplained aversion to the choirmaster. Dr Dobson was most anxious to get the heaven-sent soprano into his stalls. My mother, ever suspicious, said he only recruited me to lure Adrian in.

On Thursday mornings Prebendary Cornwell came and led the combined Juniors and Seniors of the school in a proper service instead of the usual assembly. The Headmaster was positioned alongside the Juniors to make sure we knelt, stood and sat in unison. Dr Dobson was at the piano. During one of the hymns I was mesmerised by the sight of Amos Turner chewing juicy coagulates of snot picked from his nose, and I didn't notice the Headmaster creeping up. When I felt his grip on my shoulder I quaked, thinking I was in for "the stick" and wondering 'Why me?' But

"Sing verse four solo," the man hissed.

Nerve-wracked by self consciousness, my breath came in bursts and I could only produce a mournful tremolo. Verse four seemed hellishly long, but I just managed it., and afterwards friends said I was "better than Adrian Ash".

"You weren't," Adrian himself opined, overhearing.

He was right, of course. But they wanted me to be better because Adrian "thinks he is somebody."

Later that morning Mrs Nicholas commanded me to go to the Headmaster's office to be interviewed by Dr Dobson, who pronounced himself "most gratified" by my performance. Dr Dobson was a thoroughgoing Edwardian, a walrus in a wing collar: his neck, fatter than his shiny smooth head, moved in and out of thick rings of tough-skinned flesh. He offered me "the inestimable honour" of a place in the church choir. I blushingly confessed that I could not read a score. Dr Dobson said all I would have to do was to "master the tonic sol-fa". As I stumbled gratefully to the door, the choirmaster called out,

"And have you - ahem - any young friends you think might be interested in joining us too - after a suitable audition, of course?"

"Yes." I never guessed that my mind and Dr Dobson's not to mention the Headmaster's and Mrs Nicholas's, converged on the same friend, one who needed no audition. And so one little singing fish was used to catch a bigger one but, unlike most bait, I got much benefit from the catch. At our first practice we tried on cassocks, surplices and neck ruffs, went through the tonic sol-fa, learned the basic repertoire and were duly beamed upon by Dr Dobson and Prebendary Cornwell. Behind his back, Adrian mercilessly mocked the Choirmaster, always referring to him as "The Dobsonity."

Saint Chad's church became another of my homes from home; its vestry and chancel were as a dressing-room and stage is to an actor. The Georgian nave with its gallery, where ladies sat reverently in hats, was alien territory, dark, dusty, frigid, a mere sounding box. But the all-male neo-Gothic chancel, when the morning sun made the apsidal glass glow, or when at night the interior was lit and the windows looked like shut eyelids with the veins showing, was truly what a culture is said to be: a medium of growth. Here the world of what used to be called "serious music" was made manifest: hymns, psalms, responses, and especially the sequence of Evensong: Magnificat, Nunc Dimittis and Anthem. But Dr Dobson's gown and hood as he swept his brood up the aisle wafted intimations of a world even beyond Anglican chant, for he had been taught at his Manchester college by someone who had studied in Leipzig. This "someone" had met Brahms, allowing the Dobsonity to claim an illustrious pedigree. And so, for us, even before the war was over, the word "German" came to have another significance than just that of "the Enemy".

I especially loved to hear Adrian at his piano, playing "Sleepers, Wake!" or "The Arrival of the Queen of Sheba". Adrian played them very well indeed, yet he seemed not to love them as I, who could not play at all, did. Adrian did not discriminate: he could turn his hand to all kinds of music and we seriousy discussed the relative merits of Anne Shelton and Vera Lynn. He might not have been as bright as I was in class, but he could do something far better than sums, compositions and history tests, and I was rightly in awe of him when he sat at the black and white keys and released from the queer blobs and strokes on his score sheets the spirits of the Great Composers.

We became habitués of the Victoria Hall, for oratorios sung by the galaxy of choirs (dressed to the nines but only in black and white) that existed then, for concerts given by the Halle and Liverpool orchestras, and for Brass Band marathons presided over by Harry Mortimer. Curious and exciting names became part of daily speech: Myra Hess, Clarence Raybould, Benno Moiseiwitch, Constant Lambert and Heddle Nash. Adrian took a special interest in soprano soloists, not only because they sang some of his own repertoire, but because in those days most of them had ample bosoms. However, we both agreed that the one thing most musicians lacked was sex appeal, at least until Kathleen Ferrier came on the scene. The exciting names covered a multitude of disappointing faces. I would fall in love with a recorded voice, especially a tenor's, only to find the photo of its owner a puzzling let-down.

More immediately exciting was a young man we called Ginger. We would stalk him across town and follow him into the many public lavatories he visited. For Adrian it was just a joke, but I really fancied Ginger. However, Ginger was no paedophile and saved his soulful glances only for those G.I.'s from the Red Cross who were willing to make do with what was on offer. When he became aware of being watched, he fled in terror, junior boys being much more dangerous for him than he could ever be to us.

These journeys across town were made to churches as well as urinals. Adrian would be carrying his important-looking music case, and sometimes let me carry it for him. After the time-honoured fashion he had graduated from the piano stool to the organ loft. With the blessing of the Dobsonity he was given leave to practise on many instruments dotted about the seven towns. I went along to work the hand bellows and came to know the different atmospheres and resonances and the different kinds of silence when an organ has just stopped playing, from a cold Kingdom conventicle with Wedgwood blue walls, grisaille windows and dusty stepped galleries to Anglo-Catholic basilicas with lofty candlesticks and chalky statuettes whose sealed lips seemed ever on the verge of Latin chant. Sometimes, oppressed by solitude (for the pump would be at the cramped and dusty boarded backside of the organ, and Adrian would be far away inside his diapasons) and because I felt excluded from the mystery of the staves and bar lines, I would stop pumping and the music expired in wheezy heehaws. Adrian would then wail in anguish. The only way I could assert myself was by destroying the beauty I loved, not realising that this was a normal human response called an inferiority complex. Truly I did love those burnished swells from the long gilded pipes and the architectonic order they represented and sustained. But, like the Ashes, they rendered my stature even less than it was, and I had to stand up against them sometimes.

There were dates in the calendar when attending rehearsals and turning up to two services every Sunday became worthwhile. That was when the choristers earned real money, a half-crown for a wedding or a funeral, and as much as thirty bob for the Christmas Carolling. On the nights between Boxing Day and Epiphany the choir went on its rounds. But not at any old front door. Our musicianship was reserved for pillars of the church and the associated establishment: doctors, solicitors, town councillors, funeral directors and the Chamber of Commerce. In those days such people still lived in the centre of town, in consequential houses behind rhododendron-lined front drives, among the people they served and were served by. As the Ashes appeared on this elite list, it was considered infra dig, for Adrian to join the rounds. His parents didn't want him out at night, even in his Amy Johnson outfit, and any way he didn't need the money. In his absence I got the starring soprano role.

It was thrilling to follow the leader's dimmed red lantern through the blackout, wearing gloves and scarves, processing up the select gravel, standing in the privileged porches and partaking in a ritual which embraced not only all the other choirs up and down the dark land but also the long dead in their different darkness. And it was wonderful to earn money so pleasantly, since, coming from where I did, I thought all work had to be hard. I loved especially to sing the solo as last and physically least of the gift-bearing Kings. After the gruff bass and the wavering tenor, my piping sounded more like a Virgin's than a Magus's.

And when I peered in at hallways, the banistered staircases, the gravely-pictured walls, the tawny port-coloured furniture and turkey carpets seemed like invitations to a luxurious future. Christmas decorations in these houses were always discreet yet sumptuous (evoking the pre war world), not cheap and overdone as my relatives had them. Then ladies would bring tea and mince pies, with genteel expressions of appreciation on both sides of the sacred threshold.

The lantern-bearer, the first King, was a Senior Boy: Ron Capey. His voice wavered because it had only recently broken and he didn't know whether he was going to be a tenor or a bass (nobody then referred to "baritones" in church choirs). He was a tall handsome youth, ideal for lanterns, crosses and offering plates, all of which he would carry with proud reverence as if he were the Keeper of the Grail. So reverential and stately was he that it gave his companions quite a shock one night, when we were en route between Dr Dain's and the Conservative Club, to hear him suddenly give a piercing pewit call. It did not, however, come quite out of the December blue. For it was actually an automatic response to a similar call coming from a few blocks away. Then, as if guided by the Star of Wonder itself, out of the darkness appeared none other than you, Maureen. One or two kids and dogs sidled up too, but the former drifted away, as from something corny, during the carol. You and the dogs stayed to listen.

You were lovely and Christmassy in a white scarf and white pompommed tam, and you brought a waft of Snowfire perfume, and, although you only stood there, the choir seemed to sing more lustily for your presence. You followed it then, dumbly, just as the dogs did, stopping when it stopped and standing, with your head on one side, as if hearing your master's voice. Which, in a sense, is exactly what you did hear. For it became clear that your interest was not so much in the choir as in its lantern-bearer who had conjured you up in the first place. You stood with the singers on the threshold of the Conservative Club from whose door came the smell of saved up cigars and spirits. Men in pre-war dinner jackets, with ladies in shoulder capes, a few of dark musty fur, others like furnishing material, watched the performance, waving their brandy glasses in time to the music and giving vehement "Mmmm's" at the end of each carol. And some, sentimental or sozzled or both, had tears in their eyes, especially when they heard my virgin pipe. Loyal as I was to my socialist father, I couldn't help liking these old Tories because they made such a generous contribution to our takings.

As the choir moved on to its next zone of the town, you disappeared into the night from which you had come, and it was as if a life-glow had faded. But something remained like the Cheshire cat's grin: just before you went, I saw you flash an appealing glance at Ron Capey and your lips mouthed the words, "I love you." Though the words were for Ron alone, I was as thrilled as he was. The night, the silence, the secrecy, the war, the lantern-lit lovers' faces: it was pure romance. And then, from far off, piercing invisible walls and echoing through long drab streets, came the pewit's parting cry.

All this, naturally, had to be relayed to Adrian. But I left out the mouthed words. They were a secret I shared with you and Ron, though neither of you knew I shared it.

Now Adrian clamoured to be allowed to join the carol-singing, but his parents were adamant. It was just as well, since you did not appear again on our rounds. However, as winter gave way to spring, and the evenings took on ever paler shades of pearly grey, Adrian and I kept tryst in the vicinity of the Conservative Club and tried to conjure you up, pewitting through the twilight until our throats ached. Then one night came the answer. Call by call the three of us converged. When we stood before you, you looked frankly put out and, without ceremony, demanded,

"Isn't he with you?"

"Who does she mean?" Adrian's elbow nudged me.

"How should I know?" I reddened, realising that my reply could fit both queries. "He's coming later - p'r'aps."

"P'r'aps?"

"Yes - p'r'aps."

You shrugged, pulling your cardigan tight and hugging your chest.

There was a long silence. Why doesn't Adrian say something, I wondered. I've done my bit bringing them together. But he was hypnotised by things he could not see. Then,

"How much later?" Your voice had a hard edge of suspicion and was accompanied by an irritable exhalation.

"Well - "

"P'r'aps he's not coming at all."

"P'r'aps not."

There was another long silence. Trains were heard clanking as a late blackbird on a chimney-crown came to the end of a florid solo. Your eyes scanned the distance. I thought of something.

"Adrian wants to sing to you." It was my turn to give an elbow-dig.

"I don't." Adrian dug back very sharply.

"Go on then." Your head turned to regard us, somewhat as the blackbird might have regarded a couple of worms too shrivelled to be worth his whistle.

"What shall I sing?" Adrian hissed in panic.

"Anything - a Christmas carol - "

"But it's nearly Easter."

"Then sing- er- er -I know -"Mareseadoats and Doeseadoats"."

He regularly sang this as a party piece, so it should not have presented any difficulties. He started well enough, but when he came to "a kiddleadivy too, wouldn't you?" his voice gave an asthmatic wheeze, much like the organ when I stopped pumping it. You giggled. This did not seem an inappropriate response, given the idiotic words of the song, but Adrian was mortified and, crying out,

"Oh this is awful!" disappeared into the twilight.

Still chuckling, you also departed, leaving only a whiff of scent behind you.

It took some time to restore Adrian's amour-propre, but it came about in style. One Saturday around Whitsuntide there was a wedding at church, and the choir was engaged to sing. Its treble soloist was to be paid extra. Being above money, Adrian did not volunteer; so I did. But when we heard that the bride was to be your cousin Lorna with you as bridesmaid, Adrian clamoured to take my place and I let him. This was not as selfless as it seems, for he said I could have the money. The Dobsonity was delighted, and he and Adrian had private rehearsals of "something very special". Even the money hardly made up for my sense of exclusion.

The day came and was radiant, sun flooding the chancel and nave from Saint Chad's windows and eliciting odours of arm-pits from the gentlemen and perfumed arm-pits from the ladies. Lorna looked lovely in her cream frock which had been cleverly trimmed with bits of curtain lace, and her Military Police corporal was impeccably rigid, the shiny beck of his cap seeming to push his nose into his face and his face into nonentity. This didn't seem to matter: a tailor's dummy stuffed inside a well-pressed uniform would have done for a groom. All attention was fixed on the bride, all except mine and Adrian's, that is. We craned forward from our stalls to scrutinise the bridesmaid. Your face was a picture of conscious prettiness and your bosom would have done honour to a Matron of Honour. That was how Adrian liked it, and his excitement mounted towards the moment when he would make you aware of his devotion.

It came after the nuptial solemnities when uncles were dying to get outside for a smoke and children were looking forward to the ham tea called "breakfast" in the Monica Café's Luxury Suite. But, when Adrian's soprano soared in "Where'er You Walk", it seemed as though all were rapt into the coils of paradisal longing. In those days anything by Handel was regarded as suitable for church use, and nobody present, except possibly Dr Dobson, whose organ-reeds gave a caressing pillow to the boy's voice, knew the sensual pagan context of the aria. But all must have felt the thrill of it, as Adrian directed his words in such plangent appeal to the demure and lovely bridesmaid. You knew, Maureen, though you never raised your eyes to him, you knew his pain. But did you, could you, could anyone, possibly understand the quandary you found yourself in: that of delighting in the love that was offered you, but not in the lover? Though he was an angelic vision in his perfectly fitting cassock and surplice, with his wavy hair glistening in the stained glass sun-stream, and though he had the rare gift of looking all the more beautiful when he sang, it was obvious that you were not then, if ever, turned on by angelic beauty and refinement. But you must have been, as we all are at that age and perhaps always, in love with the idea of love, and just at that moment it was Adrian who offered it.

Now he was satisfied. He had made his declaration and believed that it was secretly acknowledged. Besides, he was an artist and the response of his public ultimately meant more to him than even yours. Tears of sorrow and joy were in many eyes, and not only the women's. Adrian was the star of the show, the source of his inspiration was made subtly manifest, and the bride looked daggers as the spotlight swung inexorably away from her to you, oh Maureen, looking so worthy of devotion, just on the threshold of your womanhood.

Maureen: After and Before

Maureen: After and *Before*

"Would you care to look through her photo albums with her?" the nun asked. "Maureen and I have looked at them together - haven't we, darling? The trouble is I can't help her to put names to faces - we're not even sure which is Maureen herself on the older snaps - but if you've known her for - what was it you said?- sixty years -"

"No." He had the feeling again that they were trying to make him responsible for her. "That's the funny thing about it. I haven't seen her for fifty years. I knew her for about eight years - from the time she was ten to when she emigrated - with her husband." He emphasized the last words as if they definitively severed his own connection. Then, looking at Maureen's childishly wondering face, he felt guilty. Could those eight years have marked her life as indelibly as they had marked his? Would the photographs tell him any more than he knew?

And so they were seated side by side with an outsize tassel-tied album stretching across their thighs. He found the closeness stifling, but told himself it was like sitting with her years ago when they had read comics together. Only, she was much less interested in these snaps of her life-story than she had been in the comics.

They began, as albums invite one to do, at the end, flicking backwards. There was Australia in 1980's Technicolor, a world of determined happiness, all sunshine and surf and people at games in shorts and T-shirts, grinning from bronzed or boiled faces which he could not possibly recognise. And he soon realised that it was no use asking Maureen to identify them. Either she grimaced or smiled faintly at the image, or her eyes simply glazed, but no words escaped from her lips. All these people with whom her life had been intimately bound up were now nothing to her. Even her own image failed to register. One figure was presumably her son, the latest photographs showing him as prosperous and proprietorial with wife and young family, then each flick of the pages led one back to when he was a strapping surfing teenager. But these should-be-and meant-to-be- precious reminders raised not a flicker of recognition. She was not "Mum" or "Nana" any more. She was far far away from them in every sense.

Half-way through the album there appeared a number of snaps of a darkly handsome middle-aged man who just had to be Ray. Was his non-appearance in the later shots due to separation or death? Here nearly a lifetime was recorded, yet so much was left out, one could not piece the story together simply from the pictures. Jack slipped one snap out of its mount - the man was standing in front of a large low streamlined house with an arid-looking garden - and sure enough, on the back was written in Maureen's familiar child-like hand, "Ray at our bungalow in Berowra Heights". It was 1970.

"There's Ray."

"Ray who?"

"Your husband, Ray."

"Husband?"

"You were married to him."

"I know what a husband is. You don't -<u>you</u> never had one."

"No-I never had a husband."

"I mean a wotsit, you silly bugger." She chortled like a triumphant child.

"There's Ray again. And there."

"You keep saying that name. I wish you'd shut up." She tossed her head irritably.

Was it because she <u>wanted</u> to forget the name? It raised that troubling question again: was dementia a deliberate bid for oblivion before the body's death? Graham Greatbatch had said that Ray "led her a dance in Australia". Had she, from some unfathomable misery, cancelled out her years with him, her marriage, her son, the longest and what was conventionally thought the most important part of life? Was now, not just for Maureen but for everybody in the world, all there was? The world was weighed down with all these records of the past, all this photography so superfluous to any real need. Every room in this institution, no doubt, had its attendant albums to be got rid of along with all the other garbage at the inmate's death.

The images became easier to identify as they reached the earlier snaps.

"Here's you in a mini-skirt." This was still the Maureen he had known despite the stiff beehive hair-do.

She put her face very close to the snap whose colours had faded to a chemical-looking blueness.

"The cheeky bitch! Look at those tits. Who the hell does she think she is?"

"It's you - in the sixties by the look of it."

"In my sixties? I'm only twenty-odd now."

"No. **The** sixties. You'd be in your thirties then. Showing off your beautiful legs. You must have been glad when mini-skirts came into fashion. Did Ray take it?"

"Take what?"

"This snap."

"Who's Ray?"

"Your husband."

"If you say that again I'll smack you in the gob." In fact she dug at his ribs with her elbow.

"Hey, that comes keen."

"It was meant to." She grinned as she might have done when they were kids.

Several pages were devoted to what looked like professional studio photos, showing Maureen in a variety of glittering gowns and artificial hair-do's, a potted chronicle of fashions back from the 80's to the 50's. Usually she was squired by one dance-partner after another, men unknown to Jack. Ray was not among them. The most favoured, and obviously younger than Maureen though his age was just beginning to show in the later pictures, was a slim and rather exquisite Latin type. Occasionally between them, his arm round both their shoulders, stood an older man in a white dinner jacket, bluff, reddish, and with a mock-lecherous leer in his eye.

"I see you had a good time in Australia."

"**They** had a good time," she said darkly, jabbing a finger at the grinning images. Did she mean the men only, or was she, as before, seeing herself as another person? She put her nose close to the page and pressed her finger obliteratingly on the Latin partner.

"Who's that?" she asked.

"Just what I'd like to know. And why isn't Ray in any of these photos? Or was he the photographer?"

By way of response Maureen snatched the album and, with the clumsiness of fury, whipped the pages back to the beginning, a wholly black-and-white world. There were a few snaps recording arrival in Australia: Sydney Harbour without the Opera House but with lots of whiteness - ships, sunlight and the inevitable shorts. And then it was England, all shades of post-war grey, backyards in rare flashes of summer, the pre-fab to which Ray and Maureen had briefly moved before emigrating, and a pathetic holiday group with Blackpool Tower and the piers. Was that where they had spent their honeymoon? No, he remembered, it was on Rudyard Lake because Ray's leave was so limited, and here, from that frugal world, was just one snap to prove it. At last came the pictures Jack had been waiting for: the wedding, looking so shadowed and unlit, yet sharp, even harsh, and inescapably real - oh why was black-and-white so much more true-to-life than colour? And there was the face.

"There she is!"

"Who?"

"That woman who poked her head into the frame just at the wrong moment. Don't you remember? The rest of us moved away to let you and Ray be taken - bride and groom, just the two of you - but for some reason that old woman put her head just in front of your bouquet."

"Me Auntie Edith."

"Great-aunt, I think. So you do remember?"

"Of course I remember me own auntie."

"And the wedding?"

She frowned.

"Whose wedding?"

"Yours."

She breathed very irritably.

"Well, it wasn't yours, was it? You never -"

"Got married. Yes, you've said that over and over again. But it's your wedding we're looking at."

"Mine?"

How could a woman forget her own wedding-day? If this did not bring her back to herself, nothing could.

He scrutinized the group photograph which he had not seen for over fifty years. There were his parents, looking, though by then in their forties, still young, and Maureen's parents, she the most glamorous thing out and he sweatily handsome. Men smirked in demob suits and women simpered in costumes and court shoes and revived-looking hats. All dead. It awed him that he was now the event's sole repository, here pictured as a sort of unofficial page-boy, his insignificant pixie features pinched with April cold.

"That's me."

"Don't be daft. How can that be you?"

"I was eleven."

"You were never eleven!" She laughed scornfully.

"I had to be eleven once, to be sixty-five now."

"Sixty-five? You? Don´t be so daft.."

What did she mean? When she said "you" she must be acknowledging his identity, and her harping on about his bachelor status implied a known history behind it. Yet everything else she said was a denial of history, and of everybody's identity including his and her own.

Yet it was she who had put the albums together, lovingly inserted the snaps in chronological order, and it was her rather childish handwriting on the backs. Continuity had mattered then, a sense of an achieved past and a future still to be recorded. But now it seemed unlikely that Maureen's photograph would ever be taken again or slipped into place in her album. Now it was her mind that had been 'taken'. Was that why some religions had a rooted objection to the copying of the human image? At each 'taking' was something lost?

Now they had gone past the wedding to the few remnants of their shared world.

"Oh, there's your granddad - how it brings it all back! On his barge - see."

It was a scene from a lost paradise, a gentle old man worn by weather not stress, the canal smothered in summer flowers, blossom on the shining water, the fresh gloss of his boat and a large flower-painted jug in his hand reflecting sunlight.

Her face softened.

"Yes," she breathed. "My granddad." And she began to cry. "Why hasn't he come back for me? Doesn't he know where I am?"

"He will come," Jack said, closing the album.

Maureen: After and Before

Maureen: After and Before

As soon as you left school you started acting like a grown-up. Your mother disdained the pot-bank and soon found you a job in 'show business'. Actually, it was as an usherette and cigarette girl at the Odeon. But when you appeared spot-lit through swirling smoke - in front of the stage, between the showing of the B picture and the 'big', with the Californian sunset curtains and the Wurlitzer giving all they had got, I saw you as beautiful as any silver screen idol. The bow-tied and Brylcreamed Odeon manager, who had been one of your mother's admirers, announced, as if he were David O. Selznick and names were in his gift,

"You want to be a star, so I shall call you Stella."

It was wonderful, except that I no longer had you to go to the pictures with. Instead I had to go with your mother and Rita Philpotts (who was now Rita Alsop) and they were treated by the manager as if they were themselves stars making a personal appearance. But first I had to wait for the two women to put on their make-up, which wasn't only facial. Rita had large black-haired legs. She painted coffee-coloured stockings on them. There was a stark frontier where the brown leg fitted into the white haunch, like Italy into Switzerland. It seemed a world away from the fabled Grable legs on the screen. Rita was much more corporeal than the screen stars and was always, even in winter, "having a hot flush". She sighed a lot, missing her husband who was still, though the war had ended, "on active service in the East" (which turned out to be an airfield in Norfolk). She whiled away the heavy hours at the pictures.

One afternoon we were watching a Tarzan film. In one scene the hero is captured and put in bondage. He flexes his muscles, perspires glossily, writhes like an anaconda and expands till the ropes burst asunder and his nipples nearly burst too. Hearing heavy breathing beside me, I glanced aside at Rita, who was lit by the flicker of the screen and showed a picture as dumbfounding as any on it. Her eyes were wide, her lips were parted and from to time were washed by the tongue-tip protruding through her front teeth. Your mother chuckled sardonically to herself, aware of what her friend was going through. I sniggered in my unawareness, but I was troubled by what I saw both on and off the screen.

I experienced a more explicable thrill when Maureen became Stella and stood in a cone of light, shoulders squared in a smart white-collared, white-cuffed navy frock, against the weight of her tray. I was delighted to queue with the phalanx of smokers for my own brand of fags, made of sweet paste with orange-flavoured tips. I stood just at the tray's height, and you bent graciously down to me, your now-long turned-under hair falling forward, burnished by the spotlight, your smile worthy of immortalisation on a cigarette card.

I was fascinated by the men you were now going out with. One particularly: he was in the Royal Navy and in his Petty Officer's uniform he also looked like a film star, with his dark wavy hair and straight features, his white teeth and bedroom eyes. It wasn't long before there was talk of a wedding, though you were only sixteen. Your mother was against it:

"If I hadn't 've got married too young, I'd 've been a star by now. I don't want you to make the same mistake."

I was torn: I wanted you to be a star, too, but the films had taught me that romance and passion were essential ingredients of stardom. I wanted you to marry the handsome sailor and live happily ever after. You said you'd wait till your seventeenth birthday but no longer. It was then that you and Ray came round to our house to beg "a big favour". You wanted rooms to rent till Ray should be demobbed. Your mother refused to have you living with her because

"I don't want another man in my house - Sid's already one too many."

Although Mam was sniffy about Ray because he came from a large Irish family and his granddad had been "a Tingoleary man of all things", she had a soft spot for you and, indeed for any girl who seemed to be marrying foolishly for love. She said yes and I was thrilled. You would be there, under the same roof as I was, day in day out.

The wedding took place at the Sacred Heart church, mysterious and forbidden territory, with its grotto and Gothic presbytery attached to the church by a vaulted passage.

The lofty church over-awed me, its altar end so far distant as to seem in mist, a mist that gave off the aura of old chests in which scent-cards have been folded with the clothes, recalling long ago summers and petals smoothed flat between the pages of heavy books. Then there were the tall, tall candles, sentinels and witnesses, whose smoke whispered secrets up to God from the strange elaborate boxes, like small houses without windows, on either side of the nave. And there was the cadaverous priest who spoke to Him in a whisper too, a whistling wheezing spirituous Irish whisper, making people nudge and eye each other sideways in amused tolerance. I was perplexed by his biretta, having been brought up to think it was rude to keep your hat on in front of God - unless you were a lady, in which case it was rude not to.

Just then I wished I were a lady, for, terrific though Ray looked in his dress uniform, you looked as scrumptious as a wedding-cake in your white knee-length frock, powder blue bolero top and hair-band of artificial daisies. It seemed that on a wedding-day you just had to be a lady: the gentlemen in moth-balled or moth-eaten suits and creaking shoes looked uncomfortable and useless. I even envied Ray's two little sisters, bridesmaids officious in puff-skirted blue velvet (Ida Lidgett creations, of course), and the matrons of honour managerial in fox furs and feathered hats. Besides, if you were the bride, you were caressed and adored by everybody as if you were about to die; and then, just outside the church porch, in the caprice of April - shadow, breeze, sudden sun lighting the forsythia - you were swept into a heavenly Hollywood kiss by the handsome sailor. I knew in that instant why you wanted to be married to him. It was easy to see why he wanted to marry you: the lustrous turned-under hair innocently haloed, the expertly made-up face, the come-hither smile, the sweet-smelling curvaceous form. I couldn't wait for you both to be living under our roof, making love like Maureen O'Hara and Tyrone Power.

Then came the photo of that church-door kiss. Mamma always said it was spoiled by the face of that little old lady wearing pince-nez and a poke bonnet, putting her nose in front of the bride's nosegay just at the last minute. One wanted to look at the kiss, but one's eye was constantly drawn to the oddly angled face. It was, Mamma said, an Ill Omen. You said it was Great Aunt Edith.

The reception was held in the school canteen, whose doors kept blowing and banging as people dashed to the lavatories. We kids found it more interesting to pee against a rustic wall outside. Looking up I saw that we were doing it on the backside of Our Lady's Grotto, and I didn't know whether to feel Catholic guilt or Protestant glee. The front of the grotto was pretty with small glass jars of primroses and daffodils, and the sharp westerly whispered of Easters gone and Easters to come. The face of the Virgin was painted in a way that made her look like Olivia de Haviland as Maid Marian, so from that moment I became as mariolatrous as any Papist.

It was no warmer inside the school than out, but inside was the matrons' world where piano-keys were being tickled in Charlie Kunz-style and tea was being served, with small fish paste sandwiches and even smaller cakes, some covered in pink hundreds and thousands, others in what looked like tiny ball-bearings or silver tears. Preferring the look of the cakes but the taste of the sandwiches, I faced the sort of dilemma that has pursued me throughout life.

The men, who never seemed to be interested in food, were grouped in the makeshift bar, looking somewhat makeshift themselves. Meanwhile the women, dealing with urns and doilies, nibbled abstemiously, being in public. So the kids made up for them all, not wasting time, as they did, gossiping. But, as my mouth consumed cake, my eyes ate up the happy couple, switching from one to the other in yet another dilemma: which would I rather be?

You had a two-night honeymoon in a borrowed chalet overlooking Rudyard Lake, and the next night you brought your luscious lovemaking into the very next room to the one where Jimmy and I still shared a bed. I stayed awake as long as I could to listen, but either nothing happened, which was hard to credit, or the walls were too thick.

In no time at all Ray was back with his ship in "the Med" and you were going about the house in tears. But you had to pull yourself together to be presentable to the Odeon spotlight. As so often in the past, you let me watch you making up, and I like to think I was a small consolation to you as I had been to my mother. Your cosmetics were the latest thing, so glamorous compared with hers, and so American: Drene Shampoo, Pond's creams, Max Factor lipsticks. You sat in your amber rayon slip at your brand new utility dressing-table to put on your Odeon face. Then you reached your uniform from your brand new utility wardrobe, slid it from its satin-upholstered coat-hanger (a "personal gift" from Rita), and became the perfect cigarette girl.

The utility furniture was as exciting as the latest cosmetics - it was light-coloured and lightweight and, most important to me, it smelt of newness, of the post-war world which was just dawning on us. I would open the door of your sitting room just to smell the future, to catch the flash of chromium plate (so much smarter than brass) from tea-caddy and cruet, and the chains which held the apricot light-bowl, so sophisticated compared with the standard Electricity Company issue in the rest of the house. This, then, was what being married meant: having everything new. It must be lovely to have a complete change, nothing old remaining.

Your bedroom furniture was especially wonderful, with its matching suite instead of odd battered chests of drawers and dusty cupboards. There was a bedside cabinet in which the jerry could be stowed out of sight, not just pushed carelessly under the bed. The wardrobe soon took on your perfume, which Mamma referred to awesomely as "Four-Seven-Eleven". You opened smooth-sliding drawers to find the golden underwear, and the bed had a floral quilt with a frilly skirt, or, as you called it, "valance". People longed for luxuries and were easily persuaded to take an imitation for the real thing.

When you sank with your brand new husband into your brand new bed on the last night of his special leave, you dreamed of Ray's demob and asked God how much longer you would have to occupy it alone. You had reckoned without me.

That summer, with its luminous waiting skies and the warm hay-and-sewage-scented night air, Dadda would come home sodden with sweat from the Steel Works' unceasing furnaces. One night, when the sweat continued to ooze from him long after the rest of the family had cooled off, and he began to talk oddly, Mamma got worried and stroked his balding head with a tenderness I had not seen before and was embarrassed by.

"Is Dadda going to die?" I asked.

"Don't talk daft." But there was fear in my mother's impatience.

All through the night Dadda moaned about a cat-and-fiddle and a pony-and-trap. Mamma wasn't sure whether this was fevered rambling or rhyming slang, but when she helped him on to the chamber-pot he was taken with such a trembling that it was like trying to stabilise a half-set jelly. Then when she lay in bed beside him he perspired so violently that he soaked her too.

The next day the doctor came and diagnosed double pneumonia. His prescription was twenty-four hour nursing to be done by Mamma, and some new pills called M and B. He produced them as if they were a secret weapon and spoke with veneration of their having "worked wonders on Mr Churchill". They did the trick with Dadda too, but for three weeks his lungs hung in a balance between fire and fluid.

He had to have the bed to himself and be kept well covered despite the June heat. Mamma took over the bed that Jimmy and I shared. It was moved into the main bedroom so that she could be in constant attendance with cool head-cloths, camphorated chest rubs and the magic tablets. Jimmy slept on the settee downstairs, whilst I had a dream-come-true: *I slept with you and at your suggestion!*

"He's still only a little lad, though," you laughed, when Mamma reminded you that I was "eleven now, you know".

All day at school I kept thinking of the moment when I would slide my body between your super sheets. I couldn't understand why everything went on as normal by day when nights were so different. Our "form" moved slowly through its "periods" and "subjects", all so stiff and so different from the homely routines of the elementary school. Every now and again re-realisation flooded my being: that that night I would be sleeping with Maureen! My heart did a skip of time-nudging joy. I wanted to tell the world, but for some reason Mamma forbade the broadcasting of the information, so solemnly you might have thought it would have value for the Enemy.

It had, and the Enemy, in the form of that coarse lad Amos Turner, took full advantage. It was "break" (no longer "playtime") and a group of boys (self-conscious in new uniform) were exchanging tales they'd heard their elders tell. Amos's story concerned a drunken lodger constrained to pollute his landlady's precious Moorcroft vases in the night.

"I sleep with <u>our</u> lodger," I blurted in a bid for one-upmanship, then in horror remembered the oath of secrecy.

"Is he a boozer?" asked Amos Turner grimly, as if this would be expected.

"No - he's a she."

"Ugh!" Amos contorted his face, though it didn't really need contorting. "Women stink."

"Only old women. Maureen smells of Four-Seven-Eleven."

"Four seven eleven what?"

"It's *scent* for Pete's sake?"

"It must be for covering the stink," Amos triumphed with his grimmest smile.

"Well, *you* stink," was all I could retort.

This was feeble but true. Amos had a habit of playing with himself under the desk. Sometimes he dabbed the end of his dick with a blob of ink from his Platignum fountain-pen and produced a pungent chemical reaction.

He always contrived to have the last word. As we lined up to re-enter the school building,

"You'll have to be careful," he whispered, "and not share a dream with her."

"Why?"

"She'll have a baby if you do, that's why."

"Who's whispering?" The Duty Master inquired.

Amos pointed his thumb backwards above his shoulder, indicating anybody but himself.

When you got into bed beside me that night, I did a bit of discreet sniffing. All I smelt was Four-Seven-Eleven and the familiar Maureen smell and it was lovely. As you slid down, your slip crackled with static electricity, like the RKO mast giving off sparks. The whole world of the bedroom became suffused with filmic femininity and swallowed me into itself. All the smells were nice because they were all new: the furniture, the lino, the fluffy pink rug. There was even a lamp with a fringed shade and its own press-button switch, "something I've wanted all my life", I remember you telling Mam in one of those womanly confidences that I so often found myself sharing. And even though it had to be attached by a long looping cord to the centre light, there being no wall-sockets, it seemed the height of luxury, giving a peach glow to the room. Entering this bedroom from our part of the house was like switching from a world of grey and sepia to one of Technicolor. You - with your hair lying loose and blown on the frilly pillow, shampoo-silked as in advertisements, your amber slip held to your bare shoulders by tender ribbons shimmering and rippling like Vaseline on your olive-creamy body - represented all that was desirable in life.

But I should not have desired - and experienced - it so young. I should have been a normal boy like Amos Turner and held women in contempt. I should not have idolized the Eternal Feminine and absorbed it into my own being. And on this particular night I should not have been so tense, staying, in an agony of self-consciousness, on the edge of the bed.

"You're all right, duck," you whispered. "You can come closer. I shan't squash you."

So, in our different kinds of softness we cuddled close, and I, as the phrase would have it, nearly died. It was like being in bed with all of Hollywood at once. I wouldn't have minded if we *had* shared our dreams and produced a baby: I wanted only to perpetuate the sensation of being close to you through the brief midsummer night, during which Dadda rumbled and rambled distantly and Mamma trod the loose floor-boards to minister to him. You passed into a burbling slumber. I tried to stay awake, but all too soon there were the sparrows twittering in the guttering, bent on waking the whole world out of its bliss, and there was my bed-mate already up and dressing for her morning job at a tobacconist's. It seemed that we had only been together for five minutes.

This went on for a month, but in my memory those nights all became one, one night that grew hotter and hotter until your slip became as slippery as clear honey, and I a little fly caught in its sweet molten gold. All nights became one, that is, except one.

That night I awoke to hear a strange voice frighteningly near. At first I thought Dadda had sleepwalked into the room. But the voice, deep and distorted as it was, was female. And it was speaking right in my ear-hole. Oh heck, I thought, Maureen's raving now - has she caught double pneumonia too? Then I guessed you were having a nightmare, something I thought grown-ups didn't suffer from.

"Maureen," I called softly as from a distance, "Wake up, wake up."

Suddenly you writhed, took a great lunge at me, and I found myself on the floor.

"Don't go," you wailed. "Don't leave me."

Puzzled and unnerved, I climbed back on to the bed and you clutched me to your sweat-soaked rayon. I felt your hot tears on my face and smelt the scented ooze of your arm-pits. I could hardly breathe. Then you awoke and the grip loosened.

You lay back panting and I heard your fingers fiddle for the lamp-button. The light showed your face supported on a fist, tear-stained, bleary, even ugly.

"Oh God, I'm sorry, ducky. I had a terrible dream. I dreamt that Ray - oh Ray - was dead - his ship blew up - " You flooded with tears. I didn't know what to do or where to look. I thought of the Ill Omen but guessed it would be tactless to mention it just now.

"But it can't blow up now the war's over," I reasoned.

"You never know."

I sat against my pillow, cat-like, looking at you. You reached for a tiny hanky, embroidered with pink roses, and dabbed your nose. Then you shuffled down the bed again, leaving the light on.

"Come on - I'll be O.K. now."

I wriggled down beside you, and you did what Mamma did when I slept with her: put an arm round my belly and drew me against your lap. Again I wanted the sensation to be never-ending. You went to sleep first as usual, and I realised, thinking over your nightmare, how far from each other people sharing the same bed travel in the night. If babies came, as Amos Turner said, only from a communion of dreams, nobody would ever be born. Your arms were round me, but your dream self was with your lover oceans away.

All too soon Dadda recovered and I was back with Jimmy in the single bed. But it seemed strange now, and I felt exiled from my true centre. I pined to be with Maureen for just one more night. Dadda was a temporarily changed man, gentle and washed out, so loving to everybody, especially Mamma for her unfaltering care, that we boys looked at one another in wonder.

"Everything", Dadda promised, even putting his arm round Mamma's shoulders, "is going to be different from now on, you mark my words. No more gee-gees, no more booze-ups, I'll make it all up to you."

He really meant it and we boys, at least believed him. But no sooner had he got back to work and among his mates than he reverted to his old ways, proving what Mamma said:

"Trust men – and for sure they'll let you down."

I could only avoid letting her down by becoming a sort of woman. How could I know that that would disappoint her in a different way?

Just at that moment, to become another Maureen is what I'd have settled for. Your life seemed pure romance. Ray survived the torpedoes and, though he was not immediately demobbed, he enjoyed a lot of shore leave. Night after night you and he made love in the next room while I writhed in indefinable yearnings. And now you only had eyes for him. I put myself in your way, but you hardly noticed me.

Then, when I saw the sailor stripped to his pyjama trousers and shaving at our kitchen sink, handsome and bronzed from somewhere he referred to as a "sun-kissed paradise", my yearnings became strange and perplexing in the extreme: I fantasized a whole film scenario, in which Ray's torso would ripple in triumph over Tarzan-like bonds to gain his mate and I would lie with you both in your golden bed amidst everything that was new and clean and fresh and utterly post-war. Sometimes I crept into your bedroom and lay on the quilt to give substance to the fantasy. On one such occasion I discovered that I could produce sperm at last and had polluted the lovely golden satin. My efforts to clean it only created an obvious dark smudge. Then I remembered how my mother had typically congratulated you on your sound sense in buying a reversible quilt. What a relief! I only hoped that if you saw the smudge, you would think Ray had done it.

Then one day,

"Raymond says he's going to take me away from this bloody hole," you announced.

I was aghast, and not just because Ray was taking you away. How could he call our house that had given you your first home together a "bloody hole?" But he didn't mean the house: he meant the bit of England he had come back to from a world that had opened his eyes.

"It is a bloody 'ole," Mam agreed. "I always said we'd leave here when our ship came in. It never did of course."

But yours did, dear Maureen, and it broke my heart because it took you to Australia. That Ill Omen, your great-aunt, died and left you five hundred pounds to go with. I thought I would never see you again. And perhaps I never did, since you are not the Maureen I knew and loved so much.

Of course you were right to go. You wanted a version of the life you saw on the cinema screen, and it wasn't available in Stoke-on-Trent. By the accounts received mainly at second-hand, you "did well" in your new homeland, but one never heard accounts of those who didn't. It was like the finale of a feel-good movie: hasty comings and goings, hugging farewells, tearful promises to keep in touch, and people singing "Wish me Luck as you Wave me Goodbye" in cracked voices. I was left far behind at the end of a diminishing series of postcards. But then I began to forget you too, as my new life as a pretentious Grammar Schoolboy took over. Sometimes, though, forgetful of the time-lag, I lay awake at night and wondered whether, as your gilded body lay sleeping beside your bronzed ex-sailor, your dream-self swam the oceans to search for the little boy who had once shared - oh so much more than your bed.

"Mrs Devlin has been taken to the Infirmary. There was a sudden deterioration. They have the necessary equipment to deal with it there."

He knew what this meant.

"So she won't be coming back here?"

"It's unlikely." The nun sighed at an oft-repeated drawback to her vocation. "We shall miss her, that's for certain. But -"

Nuns and nurses, of course, weren't permitted to say that death might be the best thing even though death, in its various modes, was their business. He glanced round the room where Maureen's last bits and pieces - shoes, make-up, hair brushes, jewellery, a slip draped over a chair-back - waited in vain for her return. It seemed that even things had souls, since much-used objects looked so different from new ones.

"What becomes of all her belongings?"

"Normally, of course, the family disposes of them. But in Maureen's case we don't know yet. She would never let on who was her next-of-kin and obviously wasn't in a state to appoint one. Her closest relatives are in Australia, as you know. We have been trying to contact them."

The nun lowered her eyes as if economy with the truth had suddenly become the order of the day. At least, Jack thought, I know where one of Maureen's things must go.

"It was her wish that the cleaner - Denise - should have this mirror." He found himself staring at his own strange image in it, looking, like the room behind him, grey and forlorn. This room had briefly been the centre of the only life he now knew, where the past had continuity and a modicum of meaning. He had thought that the end of visiting a fellow human being in such a state and such a place would come as a great relief; in fact, he felt utterly bereft.

"What ward will she be in at the Infirmary?"

"The geriatric unit. You can visit her there, you know, just as you did here."

"But it won't be the same as visiting her here, will it? There was life here. She was still a human being."

"We mustn't speak of her as if she were already dead. Miracles do happen, you know."

"But not, I imagine, in the geriatric unit."

Moving from the old-fashioned Residential Home to the Geriatric Unit might have been regarded by some as a transfer from Purgatory to Heaven: a streamlined, man-made technological Heaven. Even the staff seemed to have been designed and programmed by its award-winning architect. Only the patients, for whom it had been created, sounded a sour note. They were the usual unseemly messes making hellish noises.

Jack obeyed the notice directing visitors IN THE INTERESTS OF SECURITY to check in at the Administration Desk, which was the hub of a set of pastel-washed four-bed bays and single rooms. Telephones, computers and medical machinery dominated the landscape. He was surprised to be told by the duty nurse that Maureen already had a visitor.

"But you can go in," she said in a soft African voice, directing him to one of the rooms.

He caught a glimpse of Maureen through the monitor window, which seemed to isolate her even more than did the walls. She had reached terminus now. Presumably it would have been much the same in Australia: post-modern death, a controlled process, unproblematic, without mystery. It was obvious, when he saw her propped against the pillows, that the gerontologist's prognosis had been followed to the letter: the face was small, a withered yellow fruit. Was there only one Maureen now? He had known at least four: the sunny engaging child, the teen-age dancer, the beautiful young bride, the pathetic yet feisty resident in the Home. In between the last two had been the Maureens he could never know. But now they had all come to this. Or were they all there, as in a computer which, some geek had once told him, could not lose anything, even though not everything might be retrieved on the screen?

The body still registered a drama that now went on beyond it: its breathing quick and loud, the face twitching and grimacing, the throat-muscles contracting and expanding, the hands roving round the bed-clothes as if in search of something still necessarily to be touched. Was the soul fighting to free itself while the body clung desperately to the only life it could know? Is it, he asked himself, a graphic production of the drama that is going on inside us all who feel our souls at odds with their incarnations? But does the soul really want to free itself of the body? Did not the idea of the bodily resurrection express a longing for the two to be in harmony again - or rather, for the first time?

Since he had not met any other visitor at the Home, he was expecting to find the other visitor some woman, moved by common compassion to attend the final hours of a former neighbour. He was disconcerted when a male figure rose from the bedside, tall, elderly, but still handsome, with tanned skin and a good head of grey hair.

"Ray!" The smile was unmistakable, though the teeth were now long and yellowish. "I thought you were -"

"Dead?"

"No, I mean - on the other side of the world."

"I was - till yesterday. I still feel like I'm flying. That bloody journey. It doesn't seem to get any shorter. And when I arrived, I found Mo was already on the transfer list."

He pronounced the name in an Australian way so that it sounded like Mao.

"Mo?" Jack couldn't help his tone conveying distaste for the distortion as well as for the abbreviation.

"Oh, I know you called her Maureen. I was the only one who called her Mo. Her mother hated me for it. But I was vindicated when we got to Oz - all Maureens are Mo's there."

"So d'you know who I am - not that it's all that important."

"Course I do - you're Jimmy's Jack."

Jack's reserve broke down.

"I haven't been called that in donkey's years," he laughed.

It had been the way Jimmy's pals referred to Jack, while his own referred to Jimmy as "Jack's Jimmy".

"You were Mo's Jack too, as I have cause to remember."

"Was I? Sometimes I wonder if I ever existed in my own right."

"Is that why you never married - can't say I blame you. But you meant more to Mo than anybody back here, d'you know that? She was always wondering what 'my Jack' was up to - we got really pissed off hearing about you and how clever you were."

"Must be a case of distance making the heart grow fonder. When you were on board ship she talked of nothing but 'My Ray'."

Jack did not add that in the nursing home she never mentioned him and had forgotten who he was. It seemed like a response to his thoughts rather than to his words when Ray said,

"But she never forgot you."

"We're speaking of her as if she weren't here."

"That black nurse said she can hear every word - but I've said all sorts of bloody things and there hasn't been a flicker."

"But perhaps in her soul - "

"Soul - hell! What sort of talk is that? I tell you there's nothing left in here." Ray touched - almost angrily - the lolling head, then gently pushed her shoulders back to the pillows.

Jack was abashed, as if rebuked for intellectual naiveté. He had thought he was on common ground - the Devlin family had been notoriously devout. Had Australia made an atheist of Ray? Or was being one in the first place what took him there?

"Surely you don't think that that - " Jack indicated the near-corpse - "is all there is to Maureen."

He almost laughed at himself for sounding so like one of the nuns.

"It's the brain - she's senile - demented. Everything's closing down."

"Not everything."

"Everything that matters. She wouldn't know us even if she was conscious. Isn't that the main thing - recognizing your loved ones? Did she recognise you?"

"No – yes – I don't know. Sometimes I thought she did. She knew I never got married."

"That always bothered her. I don´t know why. He's got more sense, I used to say to her."

"Did you really love her?" Jack found himself asking a very questionable question.

"After my fashion - as they say - yeah, I did - I did love her."

"She said you led her a dance in Australia." Jack tried to make the words sound light and teasing, but he was conscious of punishing Ray for not coming sooner to see his wife in her extremity.

"I led _her_ a dance?" He bent to the woman's ear. "D'ye hear thet, Mao? I led _you_ a dance! Christ! If you could only speak! Tell him that

170

isn't how it was. The shoe was on the other foot, wasn' it, Mao?"

At that point Jack remembered that it was Graham Greatbatch, not Maureen, who had said it.

A sigh came from the body on the bed and the face settled into a smile in which the dimples played as they had done long ago. Maureen seemed to be exerting her sexuality even now. Jack was disconcerted, having been brought up on the belief that women suffered more than men for love. Ray continued to address the person whom he had declared not there.

"The only thing you liked about Australia was the men, wasn' it, Mao? You never settled down there - not really. You were there for forty years and you never spoke like an Australian."

"But when I heard her speak a few months ago, I thought how Australian she sounded."

"That's because you're a Pom - like her."

"Or because the ear hears what it expects to hear." And certainly, Jack reflected, she had sounded more and more `Potteries' as she sank into dementia. He couldn't help thinking, too, that Ray had learned more Australian of circa 1950 than he needed to. Ray, meanwhile, was following his own line of thought.

"It was whinge, whinge, whinge - the heat, the insects, the shops, the fashions - just 'cause you couldn't get a New Look frock there when they first came out here. I should've known, of course. We might've come from the same spot on the globe - or should I say blot? - but that was all we had in common - the war came between us in more ways than one. When we got married I'd already seen the world. I knew what it was like living in the sun. And all the beautiful places. I knew what you people here could never know - that life was meant to be <u>lived</u> - enjoyed up to the hilt. Mo had been nowhere, nowhere. Only up and down that bloody canal with her granddad. It was asking too much of her to adapt as I did. Mind you, when I said we'd come back, she was the one who said we must stick it out. She couldn't face her mother's I-told-you-so. Who can blame her? That woman was the source of all Mo's trouble."

"She always wanted Maureen to go into show business."

"Which is just what you did, Mao, didn't you? Only it was never big-time enough for you. All those bloody dance outfits you spent your time creating when you should've been taking care of me and the boy. Dancing was what kept you going out there. You led me a dance all right. Exhibition Dancing - just the right name for it - strictly ballroom of course. I was never a dancer myself - not till the Twist came along any way and you could do your own bloody thing - so Mo found this poncy little Philippino,"

Jack remembered the lithe Latino figure in the photograph album. And beyond him, Minton, the Chinese boy. And me, he thought, why couldn't it have been me? I was her first poncy little boy. I should have been a dancer too. Why, when he and Maureen had started out from the same base, had they ended up so differently? His unlived, over-examined life unravelled before him.

"Surely she didn't - "

"What, with that little twat? I tell you he was queer as Chloe – gay, as we have to say these days. They went in for contests - and for the judges - little Poncypants Pablo was every bit as man-mad as she was - older men, business tycoons - the old men with the power - and half of them were poofs. I don't know why - she had this craving for admirers in big American cars."

"She was her mother's daughter." Jack's mind went back to the sugar-daddies who came for Cara but whose eyes and hands strayed round the nymphet who tagged along.

"You can say that again! After we moved to Berowra I couldn't take any more. It was bloody insulting - I was a good-looking guy then."

"You still are," Ray's strange look made Jack wish he had not said this.

"So what was I to do aged forty-six when she had all these wrinklies driving up to the door in their Mercs?"

"What did you do?"

"Took up with a chick of twenny-four - what else?"

"What did your son do?"

"Washed his hands of the both of us. He was grown up and working by then and living in downtown Sydney."

"So that's why he hasn't been to see his mother."

"That - and the fact that he hates this bloody country. He's an out-and-out republican - thanks to my training. He still behaves like a teenage tearaway - but he's fifty bloody years old, would you believe? Well, Mao, we can't claim to have been the perfect parents, can we? And I certainly don't claim to have been the perfect husband. But you were his mother - it's different for a man."

"Oh Ray, don't you know that sort of talk's practically illegal now?"

"No, I mean - when a man does it, it's just for fun. But a woman gives herself - too much of herself. A man can't stand seeing his wife do that for some bugger else."

A suppressed sob broke in Ray's throat and he dropped to his knees beside the bed, huddling and shuddering and hiding his eyes. Maureen's arm seemed to make a movement towards him, but then an index finger pointed as if at something in the corner of the room, invisible to the two men. Whatever it was it was real to her and seemed set to remain so into eternity. Perhaps all the "unreal" things she had seen in her dementia had also been truly there, and death was simply now the triumphant vindication of the internal world. Jack felt himself superfluous. Besides, his wrinkly bladder was demanding relief. He put a hand on Ray's shoulder and left the room.

There was a different nurse at the admin. desk. She directed him to the public toilets, which were some way off. When he returned to the desk, dutifully to sign his time of departure,

"Oh are you leaving?" the nurse asked in a tone which made him feel his departure would be a dereliction of duty, an avoidance of unpleasantness.

"I have to go." Of course he didn't *have* to. "But Mrs Devlin's husband is with her."

"Husband? Our records have her down as widowed."

"The man who was here when I came. Didn't you see him?"

"I've only just come on duty. It was Maimunah before me. P'raps she forgot to tell me." This was said with a sigh, as if at carelessness confirmed. "Let's see now," she consulted the massive documentation. "No, there's no record here of two visitors. Are you Mr Jack?"

"Jack's my Christian name."

The nurse gave a smile of necessary toleration.

"Maimunah doesn't know the difference between surnames and Christian names. She's a Somali."

"Jack was the name I gave her, Maureen - Mrs Devlin - always knew me as Jack. Are you sure there's no Mr Devlin there - or Mr Ray perhaps?"

"See for yourself - I'll just try the screen - these foreign nurses find a computer easier than pen and paper."

She fiddled and tapped and clicked her mouse, a variety of screen colours lighting her face as she tut-tutted and grimaced at her evident lack of keyboard skills.

"Nothing here," she at last concluded.

Why don't we just go and see, Jack wanted to say. What he actually said was,

"I dare say Mr Devlin didn't read your notices. He's come all the way from Australia. Things are more relaxed out there as -" he couldn't help a little dig - "they used to be here."

"Security had to be stepped up because nurses and doctors have been attacked. They'll be raping the patients next."

"I should think the terminal cases would be safe."

"Corpses aren´t even safe these days. I'd better go and check. Sometimes people claim to be next-of-kin when they're not. We don't want strange men about the place."

How d' you know I'm not strange, Jack almost said. Uncertain whether to go, he dithered as usual.

"There's nobody here now," the nurse called from the monitor window. Jack followed the voice.

"He didn't say he was leaving. I thought he'd stay till - till the end. He must have slipped away while I was in the toilet."

"I didn't see anybody leave. But I was called away from the desk after I took over."

"Well," he indicated the patient beyond the window, "we can't ask <u>her</u> where he's gone, that's for sure." Even if she knows, he added under his breath.

He entered the room where Maureen lay at peace amid the now irrelevant appurtenances of twenty-first century medical care and resuscitation. The hands had stopped roving and pointing. There was a secret smile on her face that showed the girl of fifty years back through its wizening. It was as if her body had just experienced the most blissful night of love. Was her soul perhaps uncurling from it in a whirling dance?

Jack scanned the car park in hope of finding Ray, pretending to himself that it was because he wanted to continue their conversation. In fact, it was to assure himself of the man's continued existence. He laughed at the absurdity of it. Of course he had put his hand on a solid shoulder and heard an all-too-Australian voice tell a tale which he himself could never have concocted. And besides, even the comatose Maureen had reacted to her husband's presence. But suppose she had conjured him up? It was she who had told Jack that Ray was dead. Or had she? Always there seemed to be an ambiguity about everything. Maureen saw something that only the dying or the demented could see. Perhaps she had contrived to make Jack see it too. He glanced back for reassurance at the hospital wing, its smoked glass and remote control doors, its patient- and visitor-friendly layout, its low maintenance "Japanese" gardens. In such a world the supernatural surely had no place. And yet its very technology represented man's urge to transcend nature.

He had half a mind to seek out the off-duty Maimunah for confirmation of Ray's real presence - but suppose she could not give it? He shuddered and started his car engine - better to turn his back on all this and drive home to the south coast and a world which, for him at least, was without ghosts.

That was presumably what Ray was doing right now - driving to the airport and home to Australia. It was unlikely that he would put in an appearance at Maureen's funeral.

There was only one way to find out. Besides, the whole venture would have been incomplete without the Last Respects.

But respects to what? The woman who was no longer there and couldn't give a damn? Why should anybody attend a funeral when the main person was always missing?

Ray had clearly taken this line. The only mourners were one or two cousins - Lorna, now a typical expanding widow of our time, recalled how Maureen had looked after her own mother:

"We never guessed she would come to the same end."

Which, Jack thought, was odd, considering that we all do.

The priest spoke, apparently feelingly, about someone he had never known, and so the absurd ritual went on. The box with its now unverifiable contents sank supposedly into the flames which were invisible too. Everything real about dying seemed to be kept from the spectators, who were gazing at their own futures and finding those no more real than the past or the present..

Some of us, he thought, have to wait till death to be stripped of our trappings, but Maureen's had gone long before she died. Memory, IQ, status, race, religion, the brief nationality she had resumed once and now lost again - the being Catholic or Protestant, British or Australian, the things that people made so much fuss about - all this meant no more to the demented than to the dead. We say that they have lost touch with reality when reality is precisely what they have come to: death before dying. We say they have lost all sense of time, but surely they have attained the blessed state of timelessness. And perhaps, though we say they are not there at their own funerals, they are more truly there than they have ever been elsewhere.

Yet, even through her dementia, one thing clung cheekily on: Maureen's sexuality. Was that the very last trapping that had to be put off? Or does it stay with us as we return to our Maker, or nothingness, which may amount to the same thing? Was Eve an afterthought on God's part or was sex there from the start? What did Adam do, what did he know before she materialised? The fruit of the Tree of Knowledge must surely have been a disappointment to them both. It only gave small and partial knowledge. He knew what he knew and she knew what she knew. That separate knowing and separating ignorance has persisted through all of time.